"I couldn't find [illegible] just as well, don't you think?" Joy asked in a husky voice as she answered the door wearing an old flannel shirt of her brother's.

When she moved her hand in a provocative sweep down her body, Brent unwillingly responded to the challenge in her gaze. His face reflected his awareness of her deliberate dare and made Joy feel more than a little foolish.

"I'm running a little late," she whispered. "You might like to read that magazine over there, it's one of those fix-it things. I'm fond of fixing things,' she babbled on, unable to stop herself.

"Come here, woman!" Brent commanded.

At the husky invitation in his voice, Joy almost crumpled with relief. Turning her head, she saw the tenderness and amused understanding in his eyes. She was already poised for flight, so it took merely a moment to throw herself into his arms. His mouth fitted itself to hers with a hunger she shared, and she could only cling to his neck while the floor rocked beneath her feet.

"What do you have on under that thing?"

Her breath warmed his throat as she laughed. "What do you think?"

His growl vibrated against her lips. "That's what I was afraid of. You could tempt a saint, you know?"

"And you're certainly no saint!"

"Just in case you're in doubt," he muttered, his teeth gleaming as he smiled, "I'll prove it to you. . . ."

WHAT ARE *LOVESWEPT* ROMANCES?

They are stories of true romance and touching emotion. We believe those two very important ingredients are constants in our highly sensual and very believable stories in the *LOVESWEPT* line. Our goal is to give you, the reader, stories of consistently high quality that may sometimes make you laugh, sometimes make you cry, but are always fresh and creative and contain many delightful surprises within their pages.

Most romance fans read an enormous number of books. Those they truly love, they keep. Others may be traded with friends and soon forgotten. We hope that each *LOVESWEPT* romance will be a treasure—a "keeper." We will always try to publish

LOVE STORIES YOU'LL NEVER FORGET
BY AUTHORS YOU'LL ALWAYS REMEMBER

The Editors

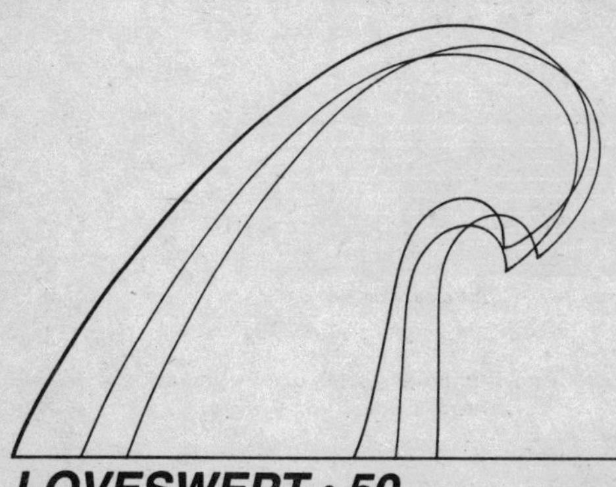

LOVESWEPT • 50

Noelle Berry McCue

In Search of Joy

BANTAM BOOKS • TORONTO • NEW YORK • LONDON • SYDNEY

IN SEARCH OF JOY

A Bantam Book / June 1984

ISBN 0-553-21633-3

Published simultaneously in the United States and Canada

Bantam Books are published by Bantam Books, Inc. Its trademark, consisting of the words "Bantam Books" and the portrayal of a rooster, is Registered in U.S. Patent and Trademark Office and in other countries. Marca Registrada. Bantam Books, Inc., 666 Fifth Avenue, New York, New York 10103.

PRINTED IN THE UNITED STATES OF AMERICA

O 0 9 8 7 6 5 4 3 2 1

One

A frothy haze covered the pale blue sky, and the sun's rays burned down on the Sacramento Valley. The heat was visible in the still air as lambent waves stacked in parallel layers from the pavement up to the horizon. There wasn't even a hint of a breeze.

Stepping into her car, Joy Barton gave a sigh of relief, which quickly turned into a groan of protest as her body touched the hot leather of the bucket seat. She rolled down both the passenger window and her own to clear the stuffy interior. As she drove, the resulting breeze played with the damp tendrils of dusky hair against her temples, and she arched her neck to encourage the welcome circulation of air.

Her long, slender fingers rapped out an impatient tattoo on the steering wheel as the Thursday-evening traffic thickened. By the time she parked her small blue Triumph in the long, curving drive in front of her parents' home, her restlessness had culminated in flagging spirits. Her mother and father were spending a week in San Francisco, and Joy had agreed to house-sit for them while they were gone. At the time she had been glad to make the offer, knowing how badly her parents needed this vacation. But after a week of roaming through the empty house, her own small but cozy apartment was beginning to seem like the pot of gold at the end of the rainbow. You idiot, she admonished herself silently. It's not that little box of an apartment you miss, but the wonderfully wet swimming pool you share with the other tenants.

A slight smile at her own folly arched her mouth, and she ran briskly up the reddish sandstone steps of the wide porch. As she moved, her cotton skirt brushed jauntily against her nylon-clad legs, and she was reminded of being only minutes away from changing into casual shorts and a halter top.

The screened porch provided welcome respite from the late-afternoon glare. But the shadowed dimness caused by the large oak tree that spread its leafy branches over most of the front yard didn't help when she was trying to find her house key. While waiting until her eyes adjusted to the light, she had her head nearly buried in her shoulder bag. Thus she failed to notice the silent figure who detached himself from the far end of the shaded porch, until a deeply masculine voice spoke from directly behind her hunched figure.

"Need any help?"

With a gasp, she whirled with such suddenness she dropped her purse directly onto two rather expensively shod feet. Lifting startled eyes upward, she noticed the knife-edge crease in the black trousers that seemed to mold themselves more tightly against long, powerful thighs than was strictly conventional. Large hands rested negligently over broad hip bones, and she was mesmerized for a moment by the black, softly curling hairs at his wrists.

Realizing her inspection had been much too thorough, Joy lifted her gaze, past the shirt that clung to the contours of a muscular chest, to his face.

The words she would have spoken remained locked in her throat as she stared in disbelief at the man towering above her. Thick black hair was swept back from a lean, tanned face. Jutting cheekbones lent a hawklike irregularity to a wholly masculine face, and only the fullness of his lower lip gave hint of a softer, more sensual nature.

"Brent?"

Her whisper was barely audible. Her body trembled, and color flowed back into her pale cheeks, as her brown eyes blazed with emotion. His steely blue eyes glinted in response, and a slow smile curved his mouth as he held out his arms. Joy needed no other urging, and hurtled her slight body at him with unselfconscious abandon.

"Brent, you've come home." She locked her hands together at the base of his strong neck and burrowed her mouth against the pulsing beat in his warm throat.

"That's some welcome, Curly Top," he gasped, gripping her arms firmly as he stepped back to inspect her features. His eyes wandered over her hair, a rich chocolate interspersed with honey-gold strands, then moved to meet her thickly lashed brown eyes, whose gold-flecked depths hinted at the passionate warmth of her nature.

"Curly Top!" She groaned, and the small dimple beside her mouth became pronounced as she pursed her lips in a teasing pout. "In case you haven't noticed, Brent Tyler, I've grown quite a lot since you last saw me."

"Mmmm, sweet sixteen, weren't you?"

"I was a rather skinny seventeen, and you know it, you beast!"

His gaze moved over her with leisurely thoroughness. "You're right," he drawled, his eyes filled with masculine appreciation. "I hadn't noticed."

She laughed, but the sound held a hollow ring. His raking inspection of her body caused tension to coil in the pit of her stomach, and the heat that surged under her skin was an alien irritation. Instantly she had to admit that the effect he had begun to have on her emotions so long ago had only intensified over the years. Desperately she sought to grasp again the instantaneous joy she had felt at her first sight of him, but the feeling was lost in the guilt of her memories. This was Brent, she thought, becoming increasingly upset as the tips of her fingers began to tingle in response to the hard arms they pressed against. With a growing sense of anguish, she acknowledged her response to his potent virility. This was her brother!

Foster brother, an inner voice mocked. But a man who had been a constant influence throughout her childhood. How dear and familiar Brent was as a boy; how well-known and well-loved he was as a young man; and how often in recent years she'd thought that Brent had vanished, to be replaced by a stranger who filled her with uncertainty.

With a muttered imprecation she bent to get her purse. She needed to move her body as a defense against the uneasiness that was tightening her nerves. After scooping several loose items back into her bag, she straightened. She only hoped he would think the color in her face had been caused by exertion.

"When did you get into town?" She was making a tremendous effort to appear coolly sophisticated, but knew she'd failed dismally when Brent muffled a laugh and brushed the back of his hand against her warm cheeks.

"I didn't mean to embarrass you," he said.

Jerking away from him, she turned her back, and sighed with relief when her fingers located the elusive door key. Brent walked over to the porch swing and picked up several pieces of luggage. He followed her inside and grinned when he saw her look of amazement.

"Close your mouth, little fish," he teased as he dropped his suitcases in the hallway with a relieved grunt. "You're seeing all my worldly goods, but don't look so disparaging. I'm damn sick of hotel rooms, and I didn't think the folks would mind if I stayed with them for a while. They've urged me often enough to come home. I would have written or called, but my decision was made on the spur of the moment. Your mother always despaired over my impulsiveness. Remember?"

The rhythm of her heartbeat increased and she took several calming breaths as he shoved his luggage against the wall. She couldn't seem to tear her eyes away from the sinuous movements of his body, until he looked back at her. The inquiry in his lifted brow sent her scurrying to close the door, her palms sliding moistly against the wood.

"Does that mean you're home for good?"

She kept her back to him, but her body felt paralyzed as she waited for his reply. Her question was met by silence, a silence that increased unbearably until it was broken by the sound of his footsteps. Hard hands gripped her shoulders, but as he turned her to face him, his eyes were gentle.

Her stomach churned with emotion. When his lids lowered to hide his brooding, thorough gaze, she knew her smile reflected her agitation. He shook his head slowly.

"Have I changed that much, Joy?"

His question held a sadness that tore at her.

She searched his face, and noticed the differences the years had brought. The lines that deepened the sides of his mouth showed the severity of self-discipline, and there was an unfamiliar harshness in his eyes. The planes of his face were more angular, almost gaunt, and beneath his eyes lingered the evidence of many sleepless nights.

As she studied him, all her uncertainties fled. Even the haunted shadows of eyes that had seen too much death and destruction couldn't suppress the man she remembered. His steady gaze held the same love and understanding she had always known from him, as well as a flicker of pain that made her ashamed of her actions.

"Yes, you have changed," she whispered, lifting a hand to trace the lines beside his mouth, "but not in any way that matters."

The tenseness flowed out of both of them as he briefly hugged her, and she was further comforted by the arm he kept around her shoulders as they walked into the living room.

"You didn't answer my question earlier," she said. "When did you get into town?"

"My plane arrived about four hours ago, and I came straight here."

"You mean you've been waiting all that time?"

He walked past her and dropped onto the couch. He looked very tired. "Don't worry, in my job I've gotten used to waiting around for something to happen." He glanced quickly around the room and smiled. "It hasn't changed much in four years, has it?"

His soft voice held a rumble of appreciation, and she grinned in response. "You know Mother! She doesn't feel comfortable unless she's surrounded by old, familiar things. Dad still insists that's the only reason she keeps him around. At least we finally managed to convince her to have the furniture reupholstered."

As she spoke, Joy kicked off her shoes and sat down next to Brent. Leaning back, she curled her legs and tucked her feet under them. "Believe me, getting her to agree was like moving Mount Everest. Dad, Keith, and I were all suffering from laryngitis and mental exhaustion before she finally gave in." She grimaced.

Brent's rich, deep laughter filled the room, echoing off the cream-colored walls. His head was resting against the brown-and-gold couch, his long body indolently stretched to its full length. She stared with unwilling fascination at the smooth brown column of his throat. Inevitably her mind wandered back to that moment of greeting when she had thrown herself into his arms. She could almost feel the brief contact her mouth had made against his warm flesh.

Clenching her teeth, she found it impossible to avert her eyes. It had been this same unthinking desire that had damaged the easy camaraderie she had known with him four years ago. Dear God! Would she never stop hating herself for the past? He had once been simply Brent, her much-loved foster brother, who had walked in and out of her life for as long as she could remember. Whenever he had come home, there had been excitement and laughter, as if a vitally missing piece of the life of every member of the family had been restored. She had so many memories of Brent holding her on his lap and ruffling her tousled curls with his hand. Why, then, couldn't she recapture the innocence of that earlier love? Why did she have to feel such sensual pleasure just looking at him? It was true that the years had changed Brent. But she realized that those changes had only heightened the already deeply-rooted attraction she felt. She hadn't been able to look at him with the uncomplicated gaze of a child for what seemed a long, long time. Instead she was seeing him through the eyes of a woman, and the thought brought with it a heady excitement. Those light blue eyes should be considered cold, she thought, but she felt as if she were burning when he looked at her. She could tell by the frown creasing Brent's face that he, too, was aware of the sensual tension she was finding it embarrassingly difficult to hide. Because of her own stupidity she was making him uncomfortable in the only home he had ever known, and the realization shamed her. Would she never learn? Taking a deep breath in an effort to control herself, she tried to wipe her face free of all expression.

She squirmed uncomfortably when he caught her staring. Quickly she lowered her eyes to her hand, as though fascinated by the movements of her fingers against the rounded arm of the couch.

"Joy, you're as jumpy as a cat on hot bricks,"

he muttered, his voice tinged with impatience. "Can't you tell me what's bothering you?"

"Nothing's wrong, Brent." Her insistence was accompanied by a passable smile. "I'm just glad you've come home." She cleared her throat. "Mother and Dad will have a wonderful surprise when they get back."

Leaning forward, he reached into the pocket of his jacket, which he had thrown on top of the coffee table, and withdrew a battered pack of cigarettes and a lighter.

"Your mother would flay me alive if she knew I was smoking in here," he mumbled as he cupped his hand around the flame. "What time will they be home?"

"They'll be back on Sunday."

"Sunday!"

She nodded. "They're visiting Keith in San Francisco. Dad's been looking rather tired lately, so Mother decided he needed to take part of his vacation early, instead of waiting for his usual three weeks in August."

"And how is our brother doing?"

She shrugged. "Oh, he's the same as always. He's working as a corporate lawyer for a large industrial firm in the city."

Brent nodded, his mouth twitching with amusement. "Your mother wrote and told me. Somehow I can't picture fun-loving Keith as a staid and proper lawyer. When I was here last, his chief interest was still girls, not law school."

Joy nodded, grinning wryly. "He was rather

frantically intense at that time, wasn't he? Mother attributes almost all her gray hairs to Keith's behavior during his years in law school, so when he comes home to visit he treads lightly. Still, I suspect that he plays the role of somber lawyer entirely for Mother's benefit. A few months ago I overheard him telling a friend that the women in the city were much more liberated than here. From the way he was talking, I gathered he likes them experienced."

Brent took a deep drag of his cigarette and exhaled slowly. He pulled her mother's favorite crystal candy dish forward and tapped his ashes into it.

"You're right," Joy teased. "Mother *would* kill you!"

He laughed, and she noticed with concern the lines of strain in his features. Even amusement couldn't entirely conceal his obvious exhaustion, and with a sense of shock she noticed faint strands of gray mingling with the black hair at his temples. She was disturbed by the bitter cast to his mouth. He looked as if his weariness were more than physical, and she felt an almost compulsive urge to comfort him.

"You look so tired," she whispered.

"I am tired," he admitted, taking another quick draw on his cigarette before putting it out.

"Now it's my turn to ask the questions." Her smile was forced, and she hesitated slightly before continuing. "What's wrong, Brent?"

"Don't worry, Joy," he muttered, leaning forward and staring down at his linked hands. "I'm just sick of the rat race, that's all."

Brent was a foreign correspondent who had built up quite a reputation over the last several years. He wrote the stories that others in his field seemed unable or unwilling to go after. His front-page stories came out of the world's trouble spots; he was one of the few reporters willing to take these dangerous assignments. And his risk-taking had caused Joy and her family a lot of worry over the years.

"You should have come home a long time ago, Brent."

"Do I detect a hint of reproach?"

She jumped, startled by the unfamiliar harshness in his voice. For the first time she saw Brent the way others must see him, as a hard man, ruthless in his determination to get to the top.

He rose to his feet and crossed the room to the window. As she stared at his back, she wondered just what he was staring at or visualizing in his mind.

"Why shouldn't I reproach you?" she said. "Four years is a long time."

She noticed that his shoulders drooped slightly, and he ran a hand across the back of his neck. Knowing his muscles must be aching with fatigue, she felt contrition at her hasty words.

Without thinking she stood, and quickly walked across the room. Her footsteps were muffled by the deep pile of the carpet. He stiffened as her arms circled his waist, and she curved her body to his to try to soothe his tension.

"I'm sorry," she said in a choked voice. Her eyes filled with tears she was determined to suppress. "I didn't mean to sound so bitchy. I've missed you so much. You don't know what it was like, hoping maybe this year you'd be able to come home for a while, only to read in a letter that you were taking yet another assignment, another risk. Eventually I tried to block thoughts of you out of my mind as much as possible."

"Maybe that was best, Joy."

"No," her voice was a haunted whisper, muffled against the broad expanse of his back. "No, because I never succeeded in blocking out the fear that I'd never see you again."

With a quiet oath he turned, and she was clasped tightly in his arms. She heard the steady beat of his heart against her cheek, and shivered when his hand reached up to cradle the back of her head.

His chest rose with a deeply drawn breath. "You're right. I should have come home a long time ago."

"Why didn't you, Brent?" She groaned and pressed her head against the softness of his shirt. "Why?"

Her question was met with an uncomfortable silence. His hesitation hinted at how much had been left unspoken between them, how many things had been left unexplained. The pressure of his hand against her neck increased. As if realizing that the fingers tightening against her tender skin could bruise as well as comfort, he moved them to her cheek. His thumb slid rhythmically against her skin as he tilted her chin. Joy's senses leaped riotously as she waited for his answer, her whole being responding to the strained silence.

"Don't you know?"

There was a glow deep in his eyes, and the intensity of it unnerved her. She shook her head automatically, even while the answer leaped quickly to mind. All at once there was vulnerable hunger in his expression, and she closed her eyes to shut out the sight of his face.

"You were in love with Beth!" she gasped, almost as if in pain.

Jerking herself out of his arms, she walked across the room and leaned her crossed arms against the smoothly carved wooden mantel above the fireplace. Remembering herself at seventeen, she knew the passionate emotions that had directed her actions that last summer had been both frightening and confusing.

That was why she had viewed his increasing closeness to the twenty-three-year-old woman next door as a defection. She had done everything she could to reclaim his attention, and eventually her efforts had served their purpose. Because he loved her, he'd given in to her demands for his time. But her selfishness had cost him the woman he loved. Beth had started dating someone else and in less than two months was engaged. The disquiet Joy now felt in Brent's company had its roots in her own guilt, but there was no way she could turn back the clock. She couldn't make the last four years, when he had roamed the world to forget the woman he had lost, disappear.

The hands that pulled her back against the warmth of a strong body interrupted her thoughts. She momentarily resisted their pressure, but the trembling in her legs defeated her.

"God, Joy," he muttered, his words muffled against her tangled curls. "Don't cry, sweetheart."

It was only then she realized her body was shaking with restrained sobs. "How can you forgive me?" she whispered miserably.

"There's nothing to forgive."

"How can you say that?"

She turned in his arms and lifted her tear-filled eyes. "If I hadn't been such a little idiot, you wouldn't have lost her."

"Hey, that's all ancient history." He smiled and brushed the tears away with his hand. "Is that the reason for these distant silences?"

"I feel so ashamed," she said hoarsely.

"You have no reason to be."

"No reason?" She pressed her hands against his chest and leaned back against his circling arms. "You couldn't stand coming home because I'd made you hate me. It was my fault Beth turned from you to another man, so don't try to protect me by denying it. Deep down inside, I think I always knew you stayed away because of me."

There was indulgence in the eyes that stared

down at her, indulgence and something undefinable that caused the breath to lock in her throat.

"You always were an emotional little thing," he murmured, bending to brush his mouth against her cheek. "I did leave because of you, but not for the reason your imagination has conjured up."

"Don't pacify me as though I were still a child!"

"Are you so much a woman, then?"

"When I was seventeen I suffered illusions of adulthood, but now I really am a woman, and I'm able to take responsibility for my actions." She hesitated, then gave in to the urge to lay her face against his chest. "I didn't want you hurt, Brent."

His hand moved through her hair, and she sighed softly with pleasure. His gentleness eased her turmoil, and with shy hesitancy she wrapped her arms around his waist. Being held in his strong clasp brought back such delightfully familiar memories, she found herself relaxing fully. Her mind seemed to cloud over and then go completely blank, and she closed her eyes to savor the moment.

"No," he muttered, "but you did want me." The arms that held her tightened. The quiet insistence in his voice pierced her lethargy with incredible swiftness, and she stared up at him. "Well, are you going to deny it, Joy?"

Two

Long, tense minutes passed, but Joy found herself unable to break the silence. The masculine certainty in Brent's eyes filled her with shame, and she felt trapped by his piercing gaze. Her long brown lashes flickered once, twice, and then stilled in a silken fan against her cheeks.

"I was a very foolish seventeen," she choked, opening her eyes and staring over his shoulder at the swirling, handmade lace on her mother's prized curtains. "At that age a girl's glands are likely to overrule her common sense, but you knew that all along, didn't you, Brent?"

"I knew you had convinced yourself you were in love with me," he admitted, his chest lifting in a tired sigh. "You were so damned young and appealing, I had the devil's own time trying to figure out how to handle the situation."

He ran a hand exasperatedly through his hair, frowning as he noticed the color tinting her cheeks. He pressed his hand gently against the warm flush, tilting her head until she was forced to meet his eyes.

"I always knew I was the reason you left home," she whispered. Through her own actions she had forced him from her life, and now that he had finally returned she realized how empty she had been without him. Without thinking, she added, "I was afraid you'd never come back, that I'd never be able to tell you how I felt."

"About breaking up my supposed romance?"

"Don't be so damned condescending," she snapped, her all-too-volatile emotions exploding in a surge of temper. "I know you cared for Beth. If it hadn't been so obvious, I wouldn't have acted like such a jealous idiot. So please give me credit for having attained a measure of maturity in four years."

Brent grasped her shoulders with a strength and suddenness that ended her tirade. "I was hoping you might have grown up in the years I've been away. I can see now I was wrong."

"That's not fair! Why condemn me for trying to tell you how I feel? You're just still not interested, are you?"

He glared at her, his superior height making her feel irritatingly vulnerable. Suddenly she slumped, and was grateful for his strength. She squeezed her eyes shut and seemed to hear her own voice from years before.

"I love you better than anyone, Brent," she had cried, wrapping her thin arms around his waist. "Do you love me best?"

"Better than anyone, babe."

She had stared at him with trust. "You'll love me best forever and ever?"

He had tenderly caressed her hair with a warm hand. "Forever and ever!" With a laugh, he had drawn a cross over his heart with a finger. "Cross my heart and hope to die."

As if he knew what memories possessed her and had journeyed with her into the past, Brent tried to comfort her. His fingers threaded through the silken strands of her hair. She tensed, caught somewhere between past and present.

"All right," he said, and bit off a curse. "If it makes you feel better to punish yourself for breaking up an imagined love affair, then by all means go ahead. But if you want the truth, then you'll have to listen to me and believe. Joy, you did not break up a love affair! Beth was a friend, and she had her own problems. If you must know, she was in love with Keith, and his running around with other women was tearing her apart."

Joy's eyes widened in shock. "Keith?"

"I guess betraying her confidence after all these years isn't too terrible; anyway, you give me no choice." Brent's mouth twisted in a wry grimace. "These last years, with all the misunderstanding and strain in our relationship, have been hell. You hardly ever answered my letters, and when you did there wasn't a trace left of my forever girl."

His words went around and around in her mind. "My forever girl . . . forever girl." Their relationship had always been so special! This was Brent the way she remembered him best . . . and yet there was a difference. Now his hand against her neck felt like a brand, and she could not express her relief by throwing herself against his solid body. She didn't dare make a move that might disrupt the tentative understanding they had reached. The child uninhibitedly would have held him close, but the woman needed to guard her actions.

"Why didn't you tell me this before?" she asked.

She waited with outward composure for his answer, ignoring the tiny flicker of annoyance in his eyes when she pressed her hands against his chest to gain breathing space.

He loosened his hold, and his eyes filled with self-disgust. "Because I took the coward's way out. As long as you imagined me in love with Beth, you weren't likely to be hurt by outright rejection. I . . . you were so damned *young*, Joy! You're trembling in my arms like a small bird trapped in uncaring hands, but there's no need, Joy."

Insistent fingers tilted her averted chin, and she was surprised by the tenderness of his gaze. Her lips shakily formed a smile, and she was rewarded for her effort when he stilled the slight tremor by brushing her mouth with his own.

"Do you remember how you used to run to me with your secrets when you were a little girl?"

"Yes," she murmured. She was spellbound by the dancing flecks lighting his eyes, and her breath caught in her throat when his grin widened as she stared. "Y-you always had time for me."

"Haven't you ever asked yourself why?"

"Because you cared for me."

He sighed; then shook his head, a bit sadly. "Oh, Joy!" he said. "You've always imagined me to be some kind of knight in shining armor, which I'm not. My ego needed your adoration a hell of a lot more than you needed the love I gave you. I've always been selfish where you were concerned. I took great care then to protect my image in your eyes, and I've taken great care since to prevent you from being disillusioned by the kind of man I've become."

"I'm not some kid addicted to fairy tales, Brent. I probably know you as well as or better than you do yourself." A frown furrowed the space between her brows. "Maybe we shouldn't focus on the past."

"But it shapes our futures," he said quietly, his smile disappearing as his mouth tightened. "Until I found a home with your family, I never fully understood such an elemental truth. When your dad found me sleeping in the orchard out back and dragged me into the house, I was a sullen sixteen-year-old, suspicious of everyone and everything around me. I sat slouched in a chair and refused to answer any questions. I wouldn't speak. I wouldn't eat the meal your mother fixed for me, even though I was starving. Your father was left with no alternative but to call the police. When they arrived you were frightened, but you didn't run to your mother to be comforted . . ."

"I ran to you." Her voice was the merest thread of sound.

He nodded. "You ran to me!"

"I—I remember when you smiled at me, I wasn't scared anymore."

He brushed a lock of hair from her cheek, grinning when it curled itself around his finger. He lifted his hand and stared at the dusky strand. "This is what you did to me that day, Joy."

He drew in his breath and laughed softly, the sound husky with suppressed emotion. "I was a runner, convinced I needed nothing and nobody, until you wrapped your arms around my neck and cried when they would have taken me away. You were just a baby, not even five years old, and yet with one glance you saw beneath the shell I'd erected, to the scared, lonely boy underneath."

A shadow of disquiet entered her eyes, and she pressed his hand against her face. "Don't, Brent!"

She was strangely hurt by the look of adoration shading his features. She was no longer that little girl who had loved him without asking for anything in return. Couldn't he see that? Now she was a woman, and yet that child he had known was forming a barrier between them.

Without looking at him, she pushed herself away from his warm body. She felt disoriented, and wrapped her arms around herself to ward off an inner chill. She crossed the room to the couch and sat down abruptly, her trembling legs refusing to hold her weight. Her shoes were lying haphazardly on the floor, and she slipped them on, frowning thoughtfully. She was burning with jealousy, shaking in the bitter aftermath of realization, as she wondered how in the world she could ever hope to compete . . . with herself.

Why did Brent have to view her actions of so many years ago as something special? Her parents had opened their hearts to him after discovering he was likely to be sent to a detention center until he reached eighteen. His record of running away from every foster home in which the county had placed him hadn't endeared him to the authorities, and the missing-person report they had filed had described him as an incorrigible juvenile. When the eldest of the officers just shook his head and stated that he doubted the boy would be given any more chances, her father had approached Brent.

"Would you like to live here with us, son?" he'd asked.

Joy had been clinging to Brent, so only she had been aware of the shudder that wracked his thin frame before he set her on her feet and rose to face her father.

"I'd like that, Mr. Barton."

John and Bess Barton accompanied Brent to the police station and were granted temporary custody. The next day they started the proceedings that would place Brent officially in their care. They were the ones who had taken over the responsibility of raising a homeless boy, not she. In her mind everything had been simple, and all she had really been aware of was having another brother to follow around.

Over the years she and Brent had shared a unique closeness, until she reached her teens. Then everything began to change. She was at first confused by the unnatural restraint in his manner toward her, then later bitterly hurt and self-conscious in his presence. Brent had destroyed the oppenness of their relationship with brutal ruthlessness, and all because he had found it impossible to put an end to her childhood!

Well, it *had* ended, and she'd make him aware of that fact before she was very much older, she vowed silently. Lifting her head, she was surprised at the intensity of his gaze as he studied her features.

"You're angry," he murmured. He swiftly crossed the room and sat down beside her. "Why?"

She was unaware of the resentment darkening her eyes as she met his questioning glance, until she saw him frown with perplexity. "You don't really want to know how I feel," she said, clenching her hands together in her lap.

"That's not true, honey."

"Isn't it?" She took a deep breath and was encouraged when his gaze seemed involuntarily drawn to the tightening material across her breasts.

He shifted restlessly, turning sideways toward her, and raising one leg until it was nearly touching hers. His hand rested over the back of the couch, and he cocked his head slightly as he looked at her.

"How do you feel, Joy?"

The thread of suppressed amusement in his voice goaded her beyond endurance. "Like a woman, not a child!"

"Are you asking me to prove it?" His eyes narrowed on her face, and she quickly averted her glance.

"What would you do if I said yes—run away again?"

"That was a low blow," he muttered.

"I know." She bit down hard on her lower lip. "I'm sorry."

He sighed. "I'm the one who should be sorry."

"The big-brother syndrome, hmmm?"

He waved a hand impatiently. "Hell, you've got me so twisted up inside I don't know what I'm thinking, let alone feeling," he snapped. "I haven't for a long time."

Her head jerked upward at the unevenness of his voice. "Then, to repeat a well-worn question, how do you feel?"

"Tempted."

"Don't tease me!"

"I wish to God I were," he whispered.

She ran her hand nervously across her skirt. Perspiration had caused the blue material to cradle her shape like a second skin. Suddenly her floral top, with its deep neckline, felt absurdly constricting, as she responded to the heightened sensuality in his gaze.

She bit down on her bottom lip and shook her head. "I wish I understood what you're trying to say."

"I was just realizing how long I've waited for this moment, Joy."

"Why?" she whispered, the tense muscles in her throat blocking her intake of air.

"Because what we think we want isn't always good for us, babe. I'm too old for you in both years and experience, but you've never been able to accept that. Somehow your feelings for me became distorted by the adolescent yearnings of a young girl eager to embrace life. Our relationship has suffered, but it's reclaimable. You brought warmth into my life, and I desperately want it back again, sweetheart. I need us to be close, and I think it's what you need, too. When the time comes for you to settle down with a decent guy who can give you the kind of life I want for you . . ."

She was suddenly furiously angry. "The kind of life you want for me?" she gasped, her expression revealing her intense frustration. "What about what I want, Brent?"

"What the hell do you think you want . . . me?" His voice was an aggravated assault on her ears, but when she winced nervously his eyes immediately softened.

"You know, I made a mistake four years ago, Joy. Before I left, I should have given you a sample of what you thought you wanted. If I had, it would have frightened some sense into you, and we wouldn't be having this conversation now."

"Why didn't you, if you're so damned all-seeing?"

She lifted her head in a gesture of defiance. Her nails were digging into her palms as she clenched her hands into tightly balled fists. "Or were you afraid?"

A muscle pulsed against his jaw. "Just what are you implying?"

She met his narrowed glance with feigned equanimity, while tension knotted her stomach. "I think you know," she whispered.

This time it was Brent who flinched, but his voice lost none of its harshness as he muffled a curse. Her light trill of laughter did nothing to reduce his anger, and she exulted in his loss of control.

"Poor Brent," she murmured, her hair swinging freely against her shoulders as she shook her head. "You didn't use Beth as a shield to protect me, but to protect yourself. You had our relationship all nicely packaged and labeled in your mind, and when I began to break free of the prescribed pattern you set for me, it nearly blew you away, didn't it? You were clever, I'll give you that. As long as I was convinced of your love for Beth, I could ignore the tension between us as something conjured up by my own imagination, but no longer. You seem determined to force me to face the truth, but I think it's time you did the same. The feeling between us came as much from you as it did from me, Brent. I can only think of one reason you didn't give me a sample—as you so bluntly phrased it—of what I thought I wanted. You were too scared of your own emotions, weren't you? Because you wanted me as much as I wanted you!"

Brent paled. At the look in his eyes her breath seemed unwilling to continue at a normal rate. Somehow it seemed to surge from her lungs at an enormous speed, and she anxiously moistened the dryness of her lips. His hand circled the back of her neck, his thumb rubbing the sensitive area beneath her heavy fall of hair.

"You did want me, didn't you?" she murmured. "You still do."

She read the answer in his eyes, and her hand lifted to his chest. She could feel the heat of his body through his shirt. Her eyes lifted to the open neck, where his tanned throat contrasted so starkly with the folds of white, and she drew in a steadying breath.

"I don't think either of us is ready for this, Joy."

His face was locked into stern lines, the muscle beside his mouth pulsating uncontrollably. She was fascinated by that telltale throbbing, and her mouth ached to savor the movement. She looked up to see his eyes staring fixedly at her moist mouth. With a muffled gasp he reached for her and lifted her across his lap. Their eyes locked together, his questioning, hers determined.

"Don't you? I think we are."

"Prove it to me," he whispered huskily.

Slowly her hand rose to caress the crisp black hair at the nape of his neck, and she closed her eyes as his head lowered. His lips moved against hers in a tentative feathering touch that left her frustratingly dissatisfied, and she spread her fingers against his hair in an upsurge of emotion. But still his mouth teased and provoked, his tongue circling her lips. He demanded her response, and she parted her lips in mute invitation.

She felt him tense, and their aroused groans mingled. He plundered her mouth with his tongue, while her body reacted to the invasion with renewed demand. He pivoted with her in his arms, laying her down on the couch and stretching out on top of her. His heaviness as he pressed against her caused her stomach to contract with unsatisfied need.

Then he was kissing her feverishly, his face beautiful with concentrated passion. He kissed her eyelids, her cheeks, her taut jaw. She tilted her head, sighing her pleasure as his tongue delved into her tingling ear. She wanted the sensations he was releasing to go on and on, until she exploded with the ecstasy rippling through her slight frame.

Her fingers moved restlessly across his strong neck, her need to touch him nearly unbearable. She moaned with frustration as her hands clenched and unclenched against his shoulders, not satisfied simply to feel those hard smooth muscles flex beneath his clothes. Lifting himself,

Brent tugged at the buttons of his shirt until it gaped open invitingly.

His whisper was muffled against her arched throat. "I want you to touch me."

She complied eagerly, sliding her palms across the moist skin of his shoulders and back and over the hair-roughened expanse of his broad chest. But now it was Brent who desired more. With a strangled cry he grasped her wrist and guided her hand into thought-shattering intimacy.

"Yes," he groaned, pressing his hips against her cupped palm. "Oh, God, yes!"

She needed no other urging, and with sensation flaring from the tips of her fingers through to the center of her being, she explored the hard evidence of his desire. He shuddered, his heavy frame pressing with renewed force against her hand.

"That's right," he gasped against her mouth, his breath blending sweetly with hers. "Oh, honey . . . don't stop!"

"Brent touch me . . . please!"

He responded eagerly to the plea in her voice and slipped her loose-fitting top down over her shoulder. One creamy breast was exposed to his touch, and she cried aloud as his thumb circled the distended tip through the lacy nothing of her bra. When his sure hands freed the front fastening, she shivered from the fever firing her blood. Completely aroused by his touch, her pinkened nipple tightened further in urgent appeal, and his ragged breathing echoed harshly in the quiet room.

"Beautiful," he said, his voice a suppressed growl.

Joy glanced down in time to see his tongue snake out to caress the peaking swell. The erotic sensation, combined with the sight of his head nestled against the whiteness of her flesh, caused her to whimper aloud the agony of her arousal. They had jumped across the wide chasm created by their past relationship with shocking swiftness, but she was more than ready to cope with the result.

She too had been waiting for these moments in his arms, with a hunger that had only intensified over the years. This was the culmination of her dreams, and she grabbed the reality with all the fervor she possessed. She felt as though her flesh had been craving the touch of his hands forever, and with innocent abandon she deliberately closed her mind to the nagging, insistent voice pleading caution. Instead she arched her body against his.

"I want you," she groaned, twisting her head from side to side. "I want you so much!"

As the sound of her voice penetrated his mind Brent sat up abruptly and ran a shaking hand over his hair. He stared down at her broodingly. The madness that had heated his blood was dying from his eyes, almost as rapidly as the hope that had flamed passionately in her heart. Only moments before she had been a woman responding to the man she loved. But reality had intruded, and she was caged into the netherworld of Brent's memory.

She tried to fill her lungs with air, for the suddenness of his withdrawal had left her shuddering. She fought her confusion as once again she was forced to hover between the woman she knew herself to be and the child he insisted she remain. She knew intuitively that he was angry only with himself, not with her, but that didn't make it any easier for her to bear.

She was proven correct when he jumped up with a curse and returned to his earlier stance by the window. His back formed a wall of isolation, and she forgot her own misery in her need to alleviate his own.

"I—it's all right," she stammered, hurriedly adjusting her clothes and rising to her feet.

"What, destroying innocence?" He laughed harshly, and massaged the back of his neck with shaking fingers. "You must be elated at how right you were. My God," he whispered, his voice terse with disbelief, "I wanted you so badly I almost couldn't stop."

"But you did stop; you—"

"I didn't want to. Isn't that enough?"

She walked over to him slowly and lifted her eyes to his. "Is that so wrong?"

"Even the look in your eyes is different," he said, almost musingly, "and I can't forgive myself for that. Sweet heaven, I must have been out of my mind!"

"None of this was your fault," she cried, cringing from his deliberate inspection of her features.

"You were a little girl playing a game, but now I've forced you to grow up in a hurry. If it's any consolation, rest assured that I despise myself. Hell, I'm a grown man. I'm supposed to have a little control."

"Brent, don't talk like that!"

Her plea fell on deaf ears. But she knew she had to make him realize how unreasonable his attitude was. "We stopped. There was no lasting harm done."

"Are you so young you can really believe that?"

"Yes, I do believe it. We kissed and touched, and I see nothing wrong in expressing our feelings for each other."

"How many men have done the same?"

"How can you ask me that?" Her voice faltered into silence when she noticed the bleakness in his eyes, and realized the trap she had fallen into through her indignation.

With a weary expulsion of breath he stilled the restless movements of her hands and looked down at their interlocking fingers. "There has been harm done, Joy. What I did was unforgivable, and I wish to heaven it had never happened!"

"Why should you wish such a thing?" she cried, violently shaking her head.

His eyes glinted with a blue fire that made her catch her breath. "It would be safer."

Her voice trembled, but she forced it into some semblance of control through sheer willpower. "Strangely enough, I fail to see any danger."

"Don't you?" He laughed, but the sound held

no amusement. "You were aroused. Do you imagine you won't want to feel like that again? It's difficult to douse the kind of fire we lighted in each other tonight, but closing our eyes and pretending to an innocence that no longer exists isn't going to solve the problem."

His sarcasm lacerated her, and she knew she had reached the end of her endurance. With a strangled sob she whirled and ran across the room. Before she could reach the door she felt his hard arms circle her from behind, effectively stopping her escape.

"Don't, Joy," he muttered, cradling her body against him. "Dear Lord, I only want what's best for you, can't you see that?"

With a sigh she leaned against him in emotional exhaustion, momentarily comforted by his tightening hold. But all too soon the muscles in his arms tensed and a new but familiar awareness flooded through her. She was powerless to stem her reaction and instinctively moved against him. Her softly rounded buttocks sought the warm evidence of his undiminished arousal as she strove to fit herself between his parted thighs. For long moments they stood swaying together in electrified silence, while all her senses reacted with a new upsurge of desire.

"Now do you understand?" He groaned, his mouth moving against her neck.

"Yes," she whispered, and closed her eyes with unbearable longing.

"Then, for both of our sakes, get out of here . . . please!"

She pulled away from him and turned, unconscious pride in her bearing. "You're the one who won't face the truth, Brent. You can place thousands of miles between us, as you did four years ago, but it won't change anything. I love you and I want you."

"Joy, I—"

"No," she interrupted, placing her fingertips against his lips. "In your mind I'm too young to make that kind of commitment, but you don't really know me any longer, Brent. I'm fully capable of making my own decisions, without help from you or anyone else. Tonight did nothing but make me certain of the strength of my feelings for you. I've never wanted any arms but yours around me, and I refuse to be ashamed of what happened tonight. The physical desire between us is too strong to be explained away, no matter how long you continue to try. It's made us strangers to each other, but maybe, in time, we can begin to know the people we've become."

She left him standing in the middle of the room, his silence following her like an oppressive weight. She could feel his gaze on her as she ascended the stairs, but she didn't turn to face him. At the moment she was too busy coming to grips with the knowledge that at long last she had finally found the courage to face herself.

Three

"Did you finish those reports for Mr. Welles, Joy?"

"They're on his desk."

Joy felt a sense of accomplishment. Too often today she had found herself unable to concentrate on the job at hand and she was all too aware of the puzzled glances Grace had repeatedly sent in her direction. Joy knew Grace was curious about her unusual preoccupation, but she simply couldn't discuss Brent's arrival with her friend.

Maybe her reticence had been the wisest decision, she thought. In the office Grace was all business, and Joy couldn't have uttered his name aloud and simply returned to her tasks. As it was, just thinking of the previous night's cataclysmic events was enough to interfere with her usual efficiency. Luckily, she had managed to place the Los

Angeles–area survey studies on Mr. Welles's desk shortly before their usual five-o'clock quitting time, feeling her efforts justified when he slid them into his briefcase and favored her with one of his rare smiles.

Realizing suddenly that Grace had said something, Joy stared blankly at the other woman. "What?"

"I said, 'Good girl,' " Grace repeated, studying Joy closely. "Norman wanted to go over those survey reports this weekend," she added, swinging a white knitted stole about her shoulders as she prepared to leave the office. "He's very pleased with your work, Joy."

"You're the one he should be pleased with, Grace," Joy admitted honestly. Getting up, she blew an errant strand of hair from her forehead and stretched her arms over her head. "You weren't too proud to stand telephone duty while I got on with it. Don't think I didn't notice your quick sleight of hand. You answered calls today before I had a chance to lift my head."

Grace sauntered to the door with her natural straight-backed glide, a slight smile her only reaction to Joy's praise. "Have a nice weekend, Joy."

Grace's words stayed in Joy's mind nearly all the way home. The closer she got to her destination, the more excited she became at the thought of a whole weekend in Brent's company. It didn't take long to park the car in the driveway, but when she began to cross the lawn her footsteps faltered. After what had occurred between them the evening before, how would he react when he saw her again?

After leaving him downstairs, she hadn't seen him for the rest of the night. She had half expected him to appear in the doorway as she put fresh sheets on the bed in his old room, but he had remained closeted in her father's den. The house couldn't have been any more silent if she were alone; and she had showered and prepared herself for bed still trying to quell the idea that he was avoiding her.

"Brent?"

Her voice echoed eerily through the hallway, and she frowned. Uneasily she called his name again as she quickly searched the downstairs rooms. The memory of his sudden departure four years ago hung heavy on her mind, and she ran toward the stairs with suspicion clawing at her insides.

"Joy! For God's sake what's wrong?"

His sleep-blurred voice came from the upper landing, and she slumped against the bannister as she fought to control her ragged breathing. His hair was tousled, and a ragged maroon robe was wrapped carelessly around his body. The look in his eyes showed his disturbed state of mind as he watched her.

"I thought you'd gone," she whispered, her wide-eyed gaze absorbing his nakedness beneath the single garment he wore with such unconscious sensuality.

"Without saying good-bye?" His mouth

twisted in disapproval. "You should know me better than that, Joy."

"I . . . you were upset last night, and this morning—"

"This morning, and for the better part of today, I've been dead to the world," he remarked, brushing one hand along his shadowed jawline. "I haven't slept much in the last week or so."

With measured steps she climbed the stairs, noting the evidence of his exhaustion as she drew closer. "Why don't you go back to bed?" she suggested in a concerned voice as she reached his side. "I'll fix dinner and bring a tray to your room."

He shook his head, his smile wry as he again fingered the stubble darkening his cheekbones. "I don't think that's such a great idea. Why don't I shower and take you out for dinner?"

"Mother left some soup in the freezer, so you won't have to trust yourself to my cooking skills." She drew in her breath, backing slightly away from him as his body warmth penetrated her senses. She looked away in confusion, well aware of the direction of her thoughts. She couldn't view his softly curling chest hair without remembering its texture against her hand, and to lift her gaze to his throat only reinforced the memory of the feel of his pulse beneath her searching mouth.

"Don't worry," he snapped, his eyes narrowing on her troubled features. "I'm not going to jump on you."

"I didn't think you were!"

He muttered something incomprehensible

beneath his breath and turned toward the bathroom. "I'm sorry," he said, swaying slightly and clinging to the edge of the wall for support. "I'm not in the best of moods right now. Just give me long enough to get cleaned up, and I'll meet you downstairs."

He disappeared through the doorway, and Joy continued on to her old bedroom. After carefully closing the door, she leaned against the wall as her disturbed pulse reverberated in her ears. Her hand trembled as she lifted it to the light switch, but she deliberately ignored this sign of weakness. She needed to distract her thoughts from the overpowering presence of the man she had just left, and with what amounted to desperation she surveyed her temporary sanctuary.

A rueful smile curved her lips. She would find no forgetfulness here, in this room she'd known as a child. Painted white, the room looked totally dissimilar to the way it had when she had first entered her teens. Then it had been all pink-and-white frills, and at the time she had thought it was the epitome of elegance.

At the end of that horrible summer, though, she had suddenly taken a violent dislike to her surroundings and decided to change the decor. The aversion had been so strong she still hated the color pink. Her feelings weren't logical; but then, she was fast coming to the conclusion that her mind just didn't function in a logical manner.

As she continued to view her old room with critical attention to detail, she grimaced. It was a study in black and white, and the results were quite startling, to say the least. Her parents had detested the change, and Joy chuckled aloud when she remembered the shocked incredulity her mother had made no attempt to hide when she first saw her daughter's new image. There were huge black-and-white throw pillows against the stark white walls, and Joy had talked her father into exchanging her French Provincial furniture for Swedish modern. This she ruthlessly proceeded to paint white with black accents. Black-and-white beads instead of traditional curtains hung at the window, and the only concession made to Bessie Barton's protest was the addition of a fringed shade.

Joy shook her head, pity in her heart for the confused and bewildered teenager who had thought to change herself by altering her environment. It was painful, remembering the child-woman she'd been. Slowly and unenthusiastically, she gathered together fresh clothing and walked automatically to the linen closet in the hallway. With towel and washcloth clutched tightly against her chest in an almost defensive attitude, she decided to use the shower adjoining her parents' bedroom.

She was somewhat refreshed by a quick wash, but as she dressed in a flared coral cotton skirt and stretchy tube top that left her gold-tinted shoulders bare, she couldn't shake off her depression. The beginning of a headache throbbed against her temples as she returned to her room, and she listlessly slipped strap-backed sandals onto her slender feet. Walking across the room, she stood and stared out her bedroom window as dusk settled into the darkness of night.

The branches of the old willow tree that dominated the back yard were still, with no trace of wind in the air to ruffle the tree's majestic serenity. Her smile was sad as she gazed at one of the symbols of her childhood. Now it no longer had to withstand the indignity of small bare feet scrambling about its limbs, or have its leaves watered with a young girl's lonely weeping. Although she had missed her brother when he left for college, Keith's departure had hardly disturbed the complacent tenor of her existence while Brent remained at home. Without her father's knowledge he had taken a job at a local garage, planning to work until he had earned enough money to finance his own education.

She clearly recalled the night Brent had dropped his bombshell. Keith was out with some friends, and the four remaining members of the family were eating dinner at the kitchen table. As young as she was at the time, when Brent pushed his plate away and asked to speak to her parents about entering the university, she had immediately sensed the tension coming from the adults.

"Damn it," John Barton protested, his chair scraping harshly against the linoleum floor as he eyed his foster son with a disapproving stare. "You have too fine a brain to waste it."

"John, let the boy speak," his wife interrupted.

Joy slipped unobtrusively from her chair and went to stand beside Brent. With a rather strained smile of encouragement he lifted her onto his lap before turning again to face her father.

"There's nothing he could say that would convince me to stand by and watch him throw his future away on a dead-end job," John blustered, glaring from Bess to Brent.

"Yes, there is, John," Bess said firmly. "I've already approved Brent's plans for the next few years, and if you give him a chance to explain, I'm sure you'll agree."

"Bessie," John muttered, his gruff voice softened with shock. "You knew about this and didn't tell me?"

His wife's face softened with contrition, and she laid a hand over John's clenched fist. "I knew Brent didn't feel right about us struggling to keep both him and Keith in college at the same time. Brent is more a man at eighteen than most boys his age, and we should respect that fact, John. He cares too much for his family to become a financial burden. You know that as well as anyone."

"I'm not trying to dampen my son's pride," John protested, meeting Brent's unreadable gaze with stoic determination. "I love you, boy," he muttered, the shakiness of his voice touching in such a large man. "I only want what's best for you."

Brent briefly rested his chin against Joy's head, as if he drew strength from her closeness. Then he began to speak, quietly at first, but then the words poured from his mouth with vibrant intensity. He talked about his past, and John and Bess were able to piece together a vivid picture of loneliness and hopeless desolation from the things he didn't say. They saw a child growing to manhood without the caring guidance he needed to make him whole, and they saw how his inner pride developed in the wasteland of unspent emotions.

John was shaken. "Why didn't you tell us before now, boy?"

"When you took me in, I didn't want anyone's pity," Brent replied. "I didn't trust the love I felt in this house. I didn't believe any of you could care for me. Anyone, that is, except little Curly Top, here." He ruffled Joy's hair, grinning when she snuggled into the crook of his arm. Then his expression sobered as his glance returned to encompass his foster parents.

"I'm not sacrificing anything, Dad." The huskiness of his voice nearly obliterated his words. "I've spent so many years in impersonal institutions, and I'm not ready to trade the only home I've ever known for another. I know I'm disappointing you with my decision to remain at home and pay board while I save for school, but I've got to do it this way. Please try to understand."

Bess turned her back and busied herself unnecessarily at the sink. John rose to his feet without looking again in Brent's direction and began moving slowly to the back door. He opened it, then hesitated, and his burly frame shuddered with a deeply drawn breath.

"I understand." His voice rasped with suppressed emotion. "And Brent?"

Slowly John turned his head, and Brent's arms tightened around Joy as he noticed the tears in their father's eyes.

"Yes, sir."

"There'll be no paying us room and board. Your help around this barn of a place will be enough. I want you to save every cent you can toward college, is that understood?"

"Yes, sir, but I—"

John interrupted Brent's protest with a sweeping gesture, then stared down at his callused hand as if he'd never seen it before. "A little while ago you called me Dad," he muttered, his throat working convulsively. "That was the first time, and I want you to know that I. . . ."

His voice trailed into silence and he slanted a rather desperate glance at his wife, who was wiping her eyes on the folds of her apron. John straightened and loudly cleared his throat. "I'd be proud of you, son, if you decided to dig ditches for a living, like your old man."

But when Joy was ten, Brent finally fulfilled John's hopes for him. He too left home for college, and Joy discovered the agony of being the one left behind. She went from adored favorite to solitary child with brutal suddenness, and even Brent's promises to send presents and letters for her alone hadn't affected her grief. When his old, personally rebuilt car was loaded and their final good-byes were being said, her father had had to pry her arms free from around Brent's neck.

With a shaky sigh Joy turned from the window. Her vivid memories created an inner restlessness she didn't know how to subdue. It took all the resolution she could muster to go downstairs to prepare dinner. Although she wasn't hungry, and she told herself Brent was perfectly capable of fixing something for himself, the thought of the lines of exhaustion that creased his face left her no alternative but to cook. When she entered the den and found him sprawled in her father's chair, his eyes closed in what appeared to be an almost drugged slumber, she knew she had been right to be concerned.

Fighting the wave of tenderness that urged her to brush a lock of midnight hair from his forehead, she hurried from the room. Once in the kitchen, she was able to put together a creditable meal of leftovers. She filled her mother's favorite enameled tureen with homemade chicken soup and set it in the middle of the glass-topped wooden serving cart. She added crusty French rolls oozing butter and heaping plates of chilled salad, and hoped the meal would be substantial enough to satisfy Brent's hunger. She wasn't worried about satisfying her own. Even the aroma wafting from the simmering soup couldn't resurrect her usually hearty appetite.

The noise of the wheeled cart being pushed across the polished hardwood floor of the hall woke Brent, and he watched guardedly as she entered the room. Avoiding his gaze, she glanced around her father's domain, and was oddly comforted by the familiarity of her surroundings. Her mind assimilated the subdued effect of wooden bookshelves, dark gold carpeting, and deep brown, heavily stuffed leather furniture.

"I see our father finally realized his dream," Brent said, breaking the tense silence.

With a sense of dismay, Joy remembered Brent had never seen this room before. It seemed wrong that Brent, so much a part of their lives, should have returned to find anything different about the home he remembered.

She pushed the cart over to the bar on the far side of the room. He was doing his best to lessen the uneasiness that still hovered between them. It wasn't his fault she found it impossible to wipe away the image of herself in his arms. Drawing a shaky breath, she strove to match his nonchalance.

"You know Dad," she murmured, keeping her back to him as she arranged their meal on top of the bar. "He always swore he would someday have a den where he could escape from screaming hordes of kids."

"He wrote and told me he was finally going ahead with his plans for adding this room," Brent remarked, getting up and moving to stand beside her. "He said he waited until we were all grown up and out of his hair, because he was damned if he was going to have your mother turning it into a playroom."

She laughed. "That sounds like Dad!"

Brent perched on the edge of one of the tall barstools. They began eating, and Joy repressed a grin when Brent quickly finished his portion, reached for the soup ladle, and refilled his bowl. Although his manners were impeccable, he devoured the meal with the eager hunger of a small boy.

"Mother wrote me too," he said with a chuckle, finally putting his spoon down. He tapped the end of the bar. "When Dad added this last piece, she was certain he was going to end up on some street corner, clutching a brown paper bag."

Joy nodded, thoughts of her parents easing her tension. A dimple formed beside her mouth, and the eyes that were finally able to meet his danced with remembered glee. "You should have been here, Brent. I promise you, it was like World War III for a while. You could have gotten marvelous inside coverage of the battles. Whenever I came home for a visit the walls seemed to ooze antagonism, and I was convinced our folks were going to end up using Keith's services as a lawyer before it was all over.

"I've never known Dad to be so tenacious about anything." She laughed. "Usually he gives in to Mother, but this time he seemed to see his resistance as a test of his masculinity. Eventually he got his bar, but the victory cost him. Mother still refuses to set foot inside the den, so Dad spends very little time here."

"That's right, you did get your own apartment,

didn't you? I remember being surprised when your mother wrote and told me you were moving out. How do you like being on your own?"

She shrugged, but her face reflected her enthusiasm. "It was lonely at first, but now I love the freedom."

His intense stare seemed to pierce her, then he lowered his gaze to the smooth surface of the bar. "No parents to hear you tiptoeing up the stairs in the early hours?"

She stiffened with anger at the not-so-subtle innuendo. "That's right," she said brightly, in a sickeningly sweet voice that would have fooled no one, least of all Brent. "A swinging single, that's me!"

"You know I didn't mean to imply anything of the sort."

"Didn't you?" she snapped. "Maybe it was better for me that you've spent the last years away from home, Brent. With your archaic view of the daughter of the house, you would have found some way to convince Mom and Dad of the unsuitability of my being on my own. But I've held down a good job for three years now, paid my rent on time, and even made ends meet enough to buy my own car."

"Joy, I—"

"And furthermore," she interrupted, her eyes shooting sparks of anger, "I'm not the naive little simpleton you think me. I don't sleep around, but don't imagine it's because I've never been asked. I've been too busy building my career to find time for an affair. I've gone from junior typist to assistant to the secretary of the president of the electronics firm I work for, and I've done it through sheer hard work. I was raised to have a sense of my own value, but I assure you I wouldn't hesitate to give myself to the man I love."

"For someone who's never shared a man's bed, you seem to be awfully sure of yourself."

"Is that the reason you couldn't finish what you started earlier?"

Joy inwardly winced at her own cruelty, but she wouldn't retreat her tormenting accusation. All the pain she had felt at the abrupt cessation of their lovemaking had coalesced into irrational indignation, and she needed to cloak a frightening sense of inadequacy.

"You're not that innocent!" Brent retorted. "I think you know I was perfectly capable of finishing what I started."

The sensuality of his words lashed at her emotions as she remembered the bold evidence of his masculinity straining against her searching hand. The desire she had felt then had been greater than anything she had ever known. But Brent was reminding her, in a hatefully cynical way, that what had been a timeless moment of discovery for her was hardly the same for him. He had made love to many other women, and the thought shattered what little composure she had.

She laughed to cover a sob. "In other words, it was just the mindless impulse of any normal man for an overeager female? Don't worry, Brent. I pride myself on being a fast learner."

His hand against her flaming cheek forced her to face him, and her eyes widened when she saw the lines of anger whitening his compressed lips. "No!" The single word, gritted through clenched teeth, sounded more like an expletive. "If I didn't know I was wrong for you, I would have taken you and damned the consequences, Joy. But you deserve more from life than I can give you. I've moved from one country to the next in search of a story, and I haven't always been the knight errant of your imagination. I exist by my own code, and when I look at you I feel shame at some of the memories I carry. In my thoughts nothing about you and the home I knew had changed, but now I'm realizing that the old expression 'you can't go home again' holds more than a little truth."

Slowly her hand lifted to twine with the fingers resting against her cheek. "Remember my saying you hadn't changed in any way that mattered?" she asked softly, lowering their joined hands until they rested on the bar between them. "It's true, Brent. The man I've always known and loved is different, the way I'm different from the young girl you remembered, but we're still the same people we always were."

She drew in a quivering breath and smiled through the tears brimming in her eyes. "And you know as well as I do that Mother and Dad never change. The struggles they've faced bringing up a family have given all of us security, even though it hasn't always been easy for them. Even their stupid battle over Dad's bar made neither of them a winner or a loser; it simply emphasized their rights as individuals."

She chuckled, relieved to see a lightening of his expression. "Frankly, if he had it to do all over again, I think Dad would make the same decision. Now when he sits with Mother in the evenings, he makes certain she appreciates the sacrifice he's making."

"I'm glad!"

"Why?" she asked gently, puzzled by the sudden haunted look in his eyes.

His mouth tightened, and he seemed to be looking inward. He was receding from her, and the bitterness in his rasping voice became the only reality.

"Sometimes I would picture them sitting on the back porch or in the living room, always together."

His voice faltered, and she could sense his frustration. "You've often needed the peace of your memories, haven't you, Brent?"

His fingers grabbed the padded leather edge of the bar. She glanced at his hands, those long, slender fingers now whitened from the force of his grip, and tentatively returned her hand to its resting place over his.

"You're home now," she whispered, her eyes filled with compassion for his obvious distress. "You don't have to hold it inside any longer."

He began to speak, releasing four years' worth of distress and disgust and fear. Joy was sickened by what she heard, but hid her reaction beneath a calm demeanor. He described a world gone mad, where staying alive was the only goal of a ravaged humanity. She was made to feel the heat of a sky reddened with flames, to hear the whining drone of bombs before they exploded, the screams of the dying.

The hand beneath hers shook, but gradually the tremors were stilled. Eventually he grew silent, his features emptying of the horror. The eyes he raised to her whitened face held a wealth of sadness, and she flinched from the isolation she felt in his glance.

"I'm sorry," he muttered.

The flush that darkened his cheekbones added to her desire to offer comfort, but the look in his hooded eyes stopped her words. He slipped from the stool, and rubbed his hand against the back of his neck. Avoiding her gaze, he cursed under his breath and began collecting the used plates and cutlery with mechanical precision. Following his lead, she helped him load the cart. Together they wheeled it into the kitchen. But when he began to roll up his shirt sleeves, she stopped him by placing her hand against his arm.

"You're still tired," she protested, a slight frown between her brows. "I'll have these finished in a few minutes, and then I'll straighten your bed so you can get more sleep. Why don't you go back into the den until I'm finished?"

"Quite the little mother, aren't you?"

She jerked her hand from his bronzed flesh as if the heat of his body had branded her, and her eyes widened with incredulous hurt at the sneer in his voice. Turning away toward the sink, she struggled to hide her vulnerability. She needn't have bothered. She heard him swear just seconds before the kitchen door slammed shut behind him.

She sighed despondently at his abrupt departure, then returned to her tasks. She managed to fill the dishwasher without dropping anything, but while she worked her mind searched for a reason for his anger. She sadly wondered if she would ever be able to unravel the mystery that surrounded him. Useless thoughts and vain conjectures chased themselves around and around in her head, and by the time the kitchen was restored to order she was no closer to finding an answer. She couldn't cope with the shifting moods of a man determined to remain a stranger. Taking a deep breath, she pushed open the kitchen door and stepped into the hallway.

"Joy, I'm sorry!"

She jumped at the sound of his voice, her heartbeat thundering in her ears. He was leaning against the wall, and from the slumped dejection of his body she suspected he had been standing outside the kitchen for quite some time. Moving away from him, she fought to swallow past the constriction in her throat and, with what dignity she could assemble, glanced in his direction.

"Just answer one question, Brent," she said wearily. "Is it me personally you dislike, or the fact that I'm a product of my environment?"

"I didn't mean—"

She whirled in place, aware that he could see the fury clouding her features. "Don't lie to me! You think of me as an unsophisticated child. While you were out writing coverage of wars and famine, I remained safe and secure in my own little world, protected from all ugliness. Isn't that how you view me?"

She didn't wait for a reply. Didn't she already know the answer? Instead, all the emotions she had repressed over the years erupted, and she gave free rein to the fears she had lived with for so long.

"Even though you imagined me wrapped in cotton wool, the ugliness still touched me, Brent. I've read every damned scrap of print you've ever written. I pored over maps, trying to trace your movements, and I could probably tell you more about political unrest in the countries where you've traveled than you could tell me."

She closed her eyes for a second, then stared at him derisively. "Do you know what it was like to be the one left behind, never knowing from one minute to the next whether there'd be a knock on the door and a telegram waiting in the hands of some impersonal messenger? Do you know what it was like to lie in my bed at night, enveloped in the darkness of my own fears for your safety? I've earned the right to share the pain of your memories, but you're so damned wrapped up in your male superiority, you just can't accept that, can you?"

She laughed, the sound filled with bitter frustration. "You're blind if you think a few minutes' of your lovemaking could strip me of my childhood!"

She drew in a deep breath, pulling away from the hand that reached out to stop her progress across the hall. Halting at the foot of the stairs, she glared back at him. "Any innocence I possessed was lost during those long nights when you were probably comforting yourself with women sophisticated enough to know the score. I used to torment myself; to imagine you running your hands over the soft skin of a faceless body, and all I wanted out of life was to be that woman. God, what a fool I've been! I've wasted four years of my life waiting for you to really see me, while you've spent those years longing to return to the adoring child you thought you knew."

Her anger spent, Joy stared at his whitened features. She had destroyed the little girl in his mind, and he refused to replace her with reality. "I can't play the role you've placed me in, Brent. I won't erase the woman I've become . . . not even for you!"

Four

Joy scowled at the squat black phone, then glumly surveyed the cluttered surface of her desk. She was falling further and further behind in her work, and she honestly didn't know how in the world she was going to be able to concentrate. Just that morning Grace had felt the need to drop a cautionary word of advice in her ear, and as her supervisor she had every right. Although during their meeting Grace used all the tact and diplomacy for which she was noted, the message had been clear.

It was the first time in her entire working career that Joy ever had to suffer the indignity of such a reprimand. She shook her head, her lips twisting in a grimace. Her honesty forced her to admit that Grace's words were long overdue . . . three weeks overdue, to be exact.

Had it been such a short span of time since Brent had returned home? She envisioned the endless parade of minutes and hours that had comprised the passing days, and sighed. Pushing her chair away from her overladen desk, she stood and began to pace restlessly across the carpeted floor. She was being eaten alive with thoughts of him. The need to haunt her parents' house in the hope of stealing a few moments with the man she loved was an ever-present danger, with only her own determination preventing her from making a fool of herself.

She snorted with disgust, while her eyes darted around her office with the nervous intensity of an animal in a cage. Off-white paint seemed to emphasize the already small dimensions of the room, and even the colorful seascape on the wall did little to lessen the office's monastic severity. Since there was no window to stare out of, her gaze clung to the picture. She would escape through the seascape! She giggled, then realized she was well on the way to becoming certified.

The image of her eventual incarceration in a straitjacket caused her to bolt across the room, where she began stuffing files in their folders without much consideration of order. She had to get out of there, and she had to do it now. Somehow she would sort out the mess tomorrow. She'd had enough for now.

Her eyes slid to the phone, and she stuck her

tongue out at it in a childish gesture of bravado. She could still hear the disappointed puzzlement in her mother's voice when she had pleaded pressure of work to turn down the dinner invitation. Had it been the fourth or the fifth time she had disappointed her parents? she wondered while stuffing the mess in her hands inside the file cabinet and locking it out of sight.

Looking one last time at her miraculously cleared desk, she groaned. Tomorrow was Saturday, and although she hated working on the weekends, she didn't have much choice. Grace had told her Mr. Welles wanted the revised contracts for a marvelously innovative energy-boosting device on his desk by Monday morning, and on his desk they would be! She hated contracts . . . she hated her job. . . . No! She loved her job . . . it was Brent Tyler she hated!

She closed her office door behind her and walked quickly through the empty building. Outside, the pavement still held the earlier, blistering temperatures of August, but as she walked the short distance to the parking garage a welcome breeze compensated her somewhat for leaving her air-conditioned office. The parking attendant saw her coming, and went to get her car. Her smile of thanks wavered slightly when he squealed to a stop practically on top of her. Denny's arrivals and departures didn't do much for her tires, she thought wryly, but it certainly felt good to be waited on at the end of a long day.

He ushered her into the car, and, as usual, the

pimpled youth's eyes wandered toward the front split in her skirt. Joy quickly suppressed a spontaneous grin before carefully seating herself and slamming the door. Denny lived for a tantalizing glimpse of thigh. On a dare, Delia, one of her friends from the typing pool, had once worn a very short skirt to work. Everyone had taken bets on whether or not Denny would run Delia's car into the side of the garage. He hadn't, but after viewing the exotic red-haired Delia in that skirt, Denny had cornered her at every opportunity. Now Delia used a garage nearly five blocks away, but she didn't seem to mind. Her long legs made mincemeat of the extra distance, and Joy secretly suspected that Delia's mornings were considerably enriched by the wolf whistles she gathered on the way.

With a wave for Denny that she felt was much too cheery for her present frame of mind, she left the garage wondering whether or not Brent was a thigh man. She mulled over the question during the short drive to her apartment complex and was still contemplating his anatomical preferences as she parked the car in its allotted slot and walked toward her apartment.

"Hey, Joy!"

She already had fitted her key in the door, but turned at the sound of her neighbor's voice. Shirley was stepping out of the pool, waving her arm with characteristic exuberance. But Joy only sighed tiredly as she watched her friend's approach. Dripping wet, Shirley's statuesque, voluptuous body shone like polished ebony. Joy groaned inwardly with ill-concealed envy. If her legs looked like Shirley's, Brent would be a thigh man, all right!

"Did you forget about the party tonight?" Shirley asked when she reached Joy's door.

Oh, hell! Joy thought. She was really going dotty if she could forget about one of Shirley's parties! Shirley was famed for them, and no wonder. The noise level alone was enough to raise the hair on your arms, and tonight would be no exception. But Shirley was smart. The festivities usually spilled over into the pool area and she invited every neighbor within hearing distance to attend. Since her guests also included the apartment manager, even when the circus lasted into the wee hours of the morning no complaints for disturbing the peace had ever been lodged.

"Oh, Joy . . . you didn't!"

With a chagrined grin, Joy nodded. "Just give me an hour to fix that potato salad I promised to bring."

"My friend, I'll give you ten minutes to don your bikini," Shirley muttered, shaking her head in disgust. "Stuff the potato salad!"

"But I—"

"I know you well enough to be prepared," Shirley insisted, a militant sparkle in her eye. "You'll spend much more than an hour on that potato salad, deliver it, stay long enough to be polite, and then spend the rest of the evening hiding in your apartment. Well, not this time. I asked

Margie and Sue to fix salads, too, so yours won't be missed by anyone but me."

Shirley sighed, a wistful expression on her face. "I love your potato salad."

"You're always flirting too much to bother eating. If you'll let me crawl into bed before twelve, I'll make a bowl tomorrow especially for you." Joy's teasing grin spoiled the sternness of her tone.

"Nothing doing! Really, Joy, when are you going to relax and enjoy life? I've invited those three gorgeous men who moved into twenty-nine last week."

Joy muttered an expletive and eyed the other woman in disgust. "Are you matchmaking again?"

"I wouldn't do such a thing!" Shirley's outraged shriek was followed by a look of assumed innocence.

Somehow Joy wasn't reassured. "You didn't just . . . hmmm . . . happen to mention me to your new friends?"

Joy's suspicions were justified when Shirley shrugged and averted her eyes. "I might have. . . ."

"Shirley, you know that——"

"But what was I supposed to do when Don asked about you?"

"Don?"

"You know, the tall redhead with the cute buns."

"I'm afraid I've never noticed a tall redhead with a cute anything," she said with a laugh, turning to open her door.

"You wouldn't!"

Joy ignored the disgruntled exclamation and entered her apartment with Shirley hard on her heels.

"You're not mad at me, are you?" Shirley asked anxiously.

"If I got angry every time you tried to fix me up, I'd have lost one of my best friends a long time ago!"

Joy crossed her tiny living room and stepped into the kitchen alcove, circling the small, free-standing bar. Glancing back at Shirley, she laughed at the other woman's downcast expression. "Come on and help me raid this place for something edible."

After Shirley left, groaning over the weight of the box of food she was carrying, Joy discarded her work clothes in favor of a gold bikini with a sheer, bat-wing-sleeved robe. As a cover-up, she decided, eyeing her slimly curved figure in her bedroom mirror, that robe left a lot to be desired. Although her suit wasn't as skimpy as Shirley's, she did seem to be showing rather a lot of smoothly tanned skin. Her eyes moved downward, and a sensuous smile curved her lips. Her thighs weren't bad. They weren't bad at all!

Exhausting hours later the party was in full swing, the combined music of stereos tuned to the same rock station blaring from more than one open doorway. Bodies were everywhere, lying on the two minuscule patches of grass at each end of the pool, in the water, dotting the pavement. With a hunted glance behind her, Joy saw the red-haired man she'd been trying to avoid for most of the evening. He was closing in fast. She stumbled into two people rapturously lost in each other's arms. In her embarrassment she clumsily backed away too quickly, and slammed her leg on a lounger holding another couple engaged in similar activity. The head buried against the man's chest turned in Joy's direction, and Shirley winked outrageously. Flushing, Joy stalked off in the general direction of the pool, careful of where she stepped. Scanning the water, her color deepened as she noticed most of the swimmers were naked to the waist, and only half of them were male.

She looked wistfully toward her door, then froze. The eyes that impaled her across the patio held an element of shock, and something else she didn't care to put a name to. When two hot hands curved themselves around her waist from behind, she shivered at the glare of disgust and fury that Brent sent winging her way.

"Finally getting to you, aren't I, doll?"

Mr. Redhead, or rather, Mr. Bighead, squeezed her waist and slid his palms suggestively downward until they rested against the top of her hips. Another tremor seized her as she saw Brent moving toward them with murder in his eyes. Frantically she tried to pry the big gorilla's fingers loose, but her struggles defeated her own purpose. She set herself off balance, and with a hot-breathed grunt the redhead pulled her back against his sweaty frame.

"Let's go to my place, doll," he said, his words slurring slightly.

But the true hunter was closing in for the kill, and in a single movement Brent reached for Joy's arm and shoved her persistent suitor into the pool. Don came up sputtering obscenities, but stopped when Brent took a threatening step forward.

" 'Doll' is going home . . . with me," he snarled, his free hand clenching into a fist. "Any objections?"

"Hey, man," the redhead whined, "I didn't know she was anyone's old lady."

By the time Bighead finished cowering, Brent had dragged Joy across the patio, thrown open the door of her apartment, and shoved her inside. The only light in the room came from a shaded reading lamp in the corner, and Joy backed in its direction with necessary haste. To her relief Brent remained by the door, his gaze roving over her like white-hot lightning.

Sometime between swimming and eating she had lost her robe, and now she longed for its scanty protection. She had dismissed Bighead's lecherous leerings without effort, but she couldn't ignore Brent's heated inspection so easily. She quailed in reaction, her skin burning wherever his eyes lingered.

"Is this how you work late?" he asked, his voice hoarse with anger.

She tilted her chin up and refused to give in to the impulse to cross her arms over her breasts, which seemed ready to spill over the top of her suit.

"I worked until nearly seven o'clock," she said tersely. "Isn't that late enough for you?"

"You told your mother you'd be stuck at the office until eight."

"What is this, a third degree?" She assumed a militant stance, her hands closing on her hips. "Is it a crime to get tired and leave earlier than I'd planned?"

"Tired, hell," he snapped, the slap of his open palm against his thigh sounding overloud in the room. "You weren't too tired to indulge in a damned orgy."

"Orgy?" she yelled, her eyes dilating with fury. "These are singles apartments, and if my friends choose to give a party—"

"There was damn little partying and a hell of a lot of rolling around going on out there!"

"I admit things were getting a little out of hand, but that's no reason for you to get all uptight. You're not so lily-white you can afford to judge my friends."

"At least I show a little discretion!"

"Oh, yes," she sneered, her jealousy erupting at the mere idea of the way he would show discretion. "You have no objection to rolling around with a woman, as long as your little games are private. Well, I happen to like my men less inhibited!"

It didn't take his enraged roar to tell her she had gone too far. His body seemed to leap across the distance that separated them, giving her no time to hurtle toward safety. Not that locking herself in the bathroom would have done any good, she thought as his steely arms trapped and lifted her in a single swift movement. In the mood he was in, Brent would have broken the door down.

When he stepped into her bedroom, conjecture on what he might have done, left her mind. All she was concerned with, as she looked into the silvered glassiness of his eyes, was what he was going to do now. She stopped struggling, every muscle in her body tensing with anticipation. Her breath whooshed from her lungs when he dropped her on the mattress, and she suppressed a chuckle of nervousness before it could escape and make matters worse.

"You're obviously hot to learn," he said harshly, "and I'm damned if you'll be taught by some bungling macho idiot who doesn't know his butt from a hole in the ground!"

"What are you talking about?"

"Why did you turn down my invitation to dinner?" he barked, changing the subject with such swiftness she frowned at him in surprise.

"Mother invited me to dinner," she argued, the frown turning into a scowl. "You're not making much sense."

"I think I'm making perfect sense!"

His jaw was so tightly clenched she wondered how he could talk, but he managed. Oh, yes! He managed quite well under the circumstances.

"I asked Mother and Dad out for a meal and suggested they call you," he continued. He glared at her even more furiously. "You would have turned me down flat, but I honestly didn't expect you to refuse your own mother. Do you think, after three weeks of avoiding me, that I haven't gotten the message? Do you think your folks aren't distressed by your behavior?"

"*My* behavior?" Suddenly her own anger more than matched his.

"You're the one who doesn't want me around," she shouted. "Did you tell them that? After your lapse from the big-brother image, you avoided me like the plague. I got up the next morning and you were gone. How do you think I felt, having to explain to Mother and Dad why you weren't there to greet them when they got home from Keith's?"

"I went to a motel for the night and spent the next day by the river. I had a hell of a lot of thinking to do, and I didn't need your help to do it."

"What conclusion did you reach, Brent? Did you decide you couldn't trust yourself around me?"

He ignored her words, but his eyes spoke volumes. With a mutter he turned his back and strode through the open doorway. She rose to her knees, aching to call him back. He was leaving, completely disgusted by the misconception he'd formed of her tonight, and she couldn't blame him. But he had had no right to leap to the worst conclusions about her, she decided, stubborn pride keeping her silent.

She was the one with the grievance, and she'd be damned if she would plead for understanding. Let him leave, and good riddance. She would return to the party she hadn't wanted to attend in the first place, and he could just lump it! Maybe the redhead wasn't so bad, after all. He probably had a lot of good qualities, if she could just find them. At least Shirley thought he had cute buns!

She was looking down miserably at her hands when she heard the metallic rasp of her bolt lock being thrown home. Startled, she lifted her head, and her glance collided with Brent's. He was slowly retracing his steps, and the intent look in his eyes made her mouth go dry with apprehension. He paused, and as if in slow motion his hand lifted to flick on the overhead light in the living room. The dark bedroom was drenched with soft shadows, creating an atmosphere of sensuous intimacy.

"I was worried about you, do you know that?" he whispered, his hands leisurely working at the buttons on his shirt.

Another button slipped through its confining hole. She had difficulty tearing her eyes away from the intriguing glimpses of black curling chest hair exposed by his dexterous fingers. But when she glanced at his face and saw his own eyes on a matching portion of her anatomy, she wished she hadn't bothered to move her gaze.

"I—I usually manage to avoid most of Shirley's parties."

As an attempt at an explanation it was pitifully weak, but she couldn't get her mind to function properly. Her breathing seemed to grow louder and louder with every casual flick of his fingers, until it roared in her ears like a freight train when he finally slipped the shirt from his shoulders.

"Do you?"

He smiled slowly, the curve of his lips matching the blatant sensuality of his whispered question. His eyes captured her, and she swallowed with difficulty. His shoes thudded as he dropped first one then the other on the carpet, and she found herself staring at the curling tendrils on the top of his head as he bent to remove his socks.

"W-what do you think you're doing, Brent?"

"You like your men more . . . uninhibited," he growled, a touch of ironic laughter in his voice. "I still can't bear to have my image tarnished, honey. I wouldn't want to disappoint you, now, would I?"

He straightened, and the blue of his eyes seemed to burn with an inner fire as he studied her stiff body. Slowly his glance touched every inch of skin exposed by her bikini, scorching her flesh as vibrantly as a touch. She had her answer, but it wasn't one she'd expected or even sought. She wanted him to desire her, but not this way. Oh, God! Not this way!

"You'll hate yourself," she whispered, her arms crossing defensively over her breasts. "You'll . . . hate me."

"I already hate myself, and I could never hate you."

He stared into her eyes as he unbuckled his belt. Although in their depths she saw a sadness that matched her own, his mouth was determined. She heard the sliding rasp of his zipper, and lowered her lashes to obscure the tempting glimpse of his hard, flat belly and strong-boned hips.

"Look at me, Joy," he murmured, his voice holding an appeal impossible to resist. "If this is what you want for us, you'll have to be the one to make the final choice."

His body was smooth golden flesh covering beautifully sculpted bone and muscle, and she shook with the need to touch him. Her glance avidly roamed over the soft black hair on his chest, following it to where it lessened across his stomach, then increased at the jointure of his thighs. There her gaze lingered, captivated by the sight of his manhood, smooth and hard and swollen with need. Her mouth went dry, and her chest ached for the release of a deeply drawn breath.

"I could have killed that joker when he put his hands on you."

She exhaled slowly.

"It was me you wanted to strangle."

He smiled, one finger lifting to trace his jaw. "Only for a moment."

"You're still furious with me."

He shook his head, his glance holding hers. "If I'm still angry, it's with myself."

"Is that what this is all about?" she whispered, her voice cracking with emotion. "Are you trying to teach me another lesson?"

"After what happened last time?" His mouth curved ruefully. "I don't have that much control."

"Why did you come here tonight?"

He hesitated, his disturbingly intense gaze dropping to her mouth. "I told myself I had to see you, to make sure you were all right."

His sudden laughter was bitter and she winced at the expression on his face. She couldn't look away, though. She was held by her response to his nakedness and his arousal, and she resented the weakness he caused her to feel. He himself seemed completely unaffected by his nudity, his stance casual, as if he were totally comfortable in his natural state. But then, he's had so much practice, she thought waspishly.

"I'm through lying to myself!"

"W-what?" The urgency of his words effectively blocked the jealous wanderings of her mind, and her eyes widened in confusion.

His hands clenched into fists.

"I need to make love to you so much I'm dying inside!"

Her breath hissed inward, while intolerable pain built inside her body. He sounded driven, as though he resented her for making it impossible for him to hide from his own desire. He had been right when he'd said they'd lighted a fire inside of each other. Now it was raging out of control, burning away everything in its path. Their past relationship was being seared into nonexistence, and she realized how desperately she needed to build a future from the ashes . . . a future with Brent!

"Do you still want me, honey?"

He moved closer, until his knees pressed against the mattress of her narrow bed.

"Yes," she whispered. "Oh, yes!"

Five

It was just one word, but it held all the longing she felt at that moment. For Joy the single utterance was woefully inadequate, and she watched in fascination as her hand moved freely down his chest. Brent stiffened as her fingertips paused at the indentation of his navel, and his swift intake of breath sounded overly loud in the muffled intimacy of the darkened room. She could hear persistent drumbeats coming from somewhere, but she wasn't certain whether the sound was caused by music or by the rapid beat of her own heart. Her fingers glided down a little farther across his stomach, and she swallowed nervously as her natural curiosity overcame her initial hesitancy.

Brent's muscles shuddered convulsively. The

betraying movement was swiftly replaced by an inner tension that transmitted itself from his flesh to her own as her fingers covered his maleness. She marveled at the soft texture of his skin, the heat that filled her palm. When his voice erupted in a groaning plea, she gasped, then whimpered in reply. Her fingers tightened, her own arousal stimulated by the throbbing evidence of his pleasure as his hard flesh pulsated against her hand.

Lost in the sensuality of her own feelings, she ran both hands over him . . . up to his broad shoulders and then down to his taut thighs. He made no move to stop her, and her excitement mounted with every sweeping caress, until touching was no longer enough. Straightening from her kneeling position on the bed she swayed toward him, her mouth lifting to press against the strong column of his throat.

His groan vibrated against her lips. As he lifted her to stand in front of him, his hands were impatient to free her from her clothing. Swiftly he released the ties that held the two scraps of material together, sucking in his breath when they fell to the floor.

"Oh, babe!" He held her away from him, while his eyes drank in the sight of her nakedness. "You're lovelier than I dreamed possible."

She captured the words to hold in memory for all time. His shaken whisper was a soothing balm to the emotions of the girl she had been, who had imagined herself alone in her wanting. So many times she'd envisioned his body at the mercy of her touch. Now, after hearing the choked passion in his voice, she knew that he had shared her longing.

With love deepening the brown depths of her eyes, she cupped his face in her hands.

"Love me," she whispered.

His long, thick lashes shadowed his cheeks as his eyes closed. Her plea was silenced by his mouth, which fastened on hers with starved insistence. She parted her lips at the prodding of his tongue, and her hands circled his waist and ran smoothly over his tightly clenched buttocks. His own hands swept down her back and matched her touch on his body by grasping the softly curving mounds. With a groan he lifted her so he could warm himself between her thighs, his ears delighting in her aroused cry as his manhood rubbed gently against the pulsing center of her femininity.

"You feel . . . so good," she cried, her head thrown back, while her hands clenched his neck for balance.

His mouth moved against her throat. "And you feel wonderful."

She had expected to feel shy and uncertain this first time with Brent, but instead discovered inside herself a sensuality that brushed every inhibition aside. She was fascinated by the texture and taste of his body, and Brent sensed her every need. With a slow smile he reclined onto the bed and pulled her on top of him.

She matched his teasing grin, her eyes brimming with laughter as she deliberately rubbed her body against his. The frustrated sound that erupted from his throat encouraged her to continue the exercise. She scooted lower, and her tongue delicately touched the hard tip of his masculine nipple.

"Who taught you to do that?" His voice was a strangled growl.

She lifted her head, her eyes soft and luminous as she recognized the barely restrained pleasure in his. "You did," she teased. "Don't you remember?"

"I think I remember every minute I ever spent with you," he said, his large hands framing her face.

"I wish you'd forget all the times I drove you crazy."

"Like now?" he murmured.

His eyes lighted with arousal as he deliberately flexed his hips and gently coaxed her onto her back. With his lips and tongue he began a slow exploration of her flesh. She clutched at him helplessly, unable to contain her low moan of desire.

"It's my turn to drive you crazy." He laughed, his breath warm against the soft flesh of her gently curving stomach. His eyes held hers for a long, tension-filled moment before he deliberately moved his mouth even lower.

With a startled cry she arched to meet the sweep of his tongue, her eyes closing in ecstasy. He teased and tasted and devoured the fluidity of her uncontrollable response, until with unintelligible cries she pleaded for an end to the pressure building inside of her.

His chest was heaving, his eyes flickers of blue fire as he moved over her. He parted her thighs and placed his hands beside her twisting head. His mouth found her breasts, savoring each in turn.

In a frenzy of need, she curved her arms around his shoulders. Her nails scoured the skin of his back, and she heard his breathing escalate until it matched the rhythm of her own hurried pants.

"Now," he muttered, clutching her hair in his hands until the restless movements of her head were stilled. "I've got to take you now!"

Gently he teased her lips apart in a brief kiss and began carefully to enter her. "Don't close your eyes, honey," he gasped. "I want to see myself in them."

When her lids lifted, she found herself trapped inside a feeling so powerful, she felt their souls must be merging. He was careful and slow, and the feel of him inside of her made her shake with pleasure. The pain she had expected was so brief she barely had time to react. Brent waited until she had adjusted to him, and then began to move.

"Am I hurting you?" he whispered.

Her eyes wide and startled, she wrapped her legs around his lean hips. "No," she groaned. "Oh, no!"

His face reflected the expression in her eyes.

"That's right, honey. Move with me, stay with me all the way."

She had no choice. She was caught up in the exquisite sensations flaring between them, her whole being concentrating on the quivering pressure that was demanding release.

"Good girl," he crooned, his mouth against her throat. "Let go, babe."

As though his voice were a trigger freeing her emotions, she spilled over into a spiraling delight she had never dreamed possible. She cried aloud, and her own voice chanting his name sent Brent over the threshold of pleasure. For an eternity they were joined in a world of their making, until they both floated into an aftermath of satiated relaxation.

Eventually Brent's breathing slowed, and he curved her closely to his side. "Are you all right?"

Joy's arms tightened around him, her hold a silken bond of entrapment. "I'm wonderful!"

Lifting his head, Brent pressed soft, delicate kisses against the trembling fan of lashes that hid her eyes from him. "I'm not disputing that," he murmured huskily. "But making love for the first time isn't always the most pleasant experience for a woman."

"It's all relative, Watson," she quipped, enjoying the feel of his mat of chest hair against her lips as she spoke.

"You just made love with Brent," he teased, placing a well-aimed swat against her exposed rear. "Who's this guy Watson?"

"One of my many lovers," she said, her tongue flicking out to taste the skin at the base of his throat.

"Mmmm, hungry little thing, aren't you?" He accommodatingly tilted his head back to further indulge her appetite.

"Is it my fault you taste delicious?"

"You're the one who nearly got eaten alive." He grinned, and his voice was raspy with remembered pleasure. "I tried to be gentle, but for a while there I went completely out of my mind."

He searched her eyes, his expression concerned. "Did I hurt you badly, love?"

She could feel the heat rising in her face at his bluntness, but she held his gaze with the confidence he had given her in her womanhood. "This was my first time," she whispered, "but I found the experience everything I'd dreamed it could be. My lover was kind, and considerate enough of my feelings to be certain I was ready before he took me."

Brent's eyes glowed, and in an excess of emotion he reached for her, cradling her so that her head rested in the hollow of his throat. "I love you so much, Joy."

Her fingers gently traced his firm mouth. "You couldn't love me any more than I love you."

He chuckled endearingly when she peeked up at him, and threaded his fingers through her tousled hair. "That point's debatable."

"Not to me!"

Held snugly against the warmth of his body,

Joy felt her lids begin to droop. Before she could prevent it, a yawn escaped, quickly followed by another. She felt Brent's laughter through her own body and languidly entwined her legs with his. She was warm and safe, and very much loved, when sleep finally descended on them both.

Joy was in the midst of a delicious dream, and although she sensed it was morning she was reluctant to relinquish her fantasy. A warm mouth teased the corners of her lips until they quirked upward in a smile, and her body absorbed the reality of Brent's presence in her bed with almost delirious happiness. She was too relaxed to mutter even the tiniest protest when he shifted into a sitting position and pulled her up with him.

"Maybe if I feed you I'll be able to get you to open those beautiful brown eyes of yours," he whispered.

She couldn't make herself do his bidding, but did at least manage to reach out for him with her hands. "Why don't we stay here a little longer?"

"Don't tempt me, woman," he growled, planting a kiss on the tip of her nose. "I don't want to leave this warm bed any more than you do, but a glorious day awaits my lady. Let's spend it together and take a drive around some of our old haunts."

At this her eyes did fly open. "Oh, I can't," she cried, disappointment clouding her features. "I have to go in to work. Grace mentioned coming in for a few hours to help me, so I can't avoid it.

"For some strange reason I simply can't, for the life of me, fathom," she teased, slanting him a look out of the corners of her eyes, "I've been having trouble concentrating lately."

"How long do you think it'll take?"

She smiled at the disappointment in his voice. "If I can make myself get up,"—she sighed, glancing at her nightstand clock—"I might be able to make it to the office by nine. If I finish up around four, that should be long enough to appease my conscience."

He grimaced, his expression sobering abruptly as he looked down at her. "I wish mine could be appeased so easily."

At the sudden seriousness in his voice, her body jerked as though it had been touched with a hot wire. A gamut of emotions chased across his face. She was able to discern worry and sadness, but what was unbearable was a lingering hint of remorse.

"What we shared together was perfect," she gasped, her mouth trembling. "Please don't spoil it, Brent!"

His expression darkened, and a haunted look entered his eyes. "I wish I could be the perfect man for you, but you deserve so much better, babe."

"Is that what you think I want . . . perfection?"

He leaned against the headboard of the bed with closed eyes. "I don't know what I think anymore." He sighed dispiritedly. "Yesterday I would have thought myself incapable of forcing myself into your bed."

"You didn't force yourself," she exclaimed indignantly.

"Damn it, you were a total innocent," he said desperately. "I can't help hating myself for using my experience to gain a response from you. I had no right pressing you into a physical relationship before making sure you were ready for the emotional repercussions. With any other woman this would be enough, but never with you!

"I'd planned on giving you time to begin to know me as I am now," he continued, "and giving in to my desire for you is bound to complicate matters. No matter how much you might argue the point, you're going to have to come to terms with what loving me would mean. My career is a part of the man I am, and you'd have to put up with being left alone a great deal of the time."

He reacted to her shocked expression with a muffled expletive and pulled her with him when he rose to his feet. She shivered against the hands that gripped her shoulders. "It's a little late to indulge in postmortems," she whispered.

Sliding his hands through her hair, he pulled her into his arms. "I only pray it isn't too late to salvage something from this situation."

With a choked cry she pressed her head against his chest, and closed her eyes as she remembered the way she had taunted him. "I happen to like my men less . . . inhibited," she had said.

Her irresponsible words to him returned to haunt her, now, when she was at her most vulnerable. The memory stripped her of all pretense, and she didn't like the image of herself that arose in her mind. She had played with his emotions the way a child would with a toy, without once considering how responsible he would feel afterward. Only now, she was beginning to realize that there was more to loving someone than just saying the words, and the knowledge was frightening. Brent was as vulnerable to her as she was to him, and it was this vulnerability that had to be carefully guarded against harm.

She extricated herself from his arms, and walked to the closet to get her robe. She could sense that his gaze followed her, and felt a twist of cynicism. How strange to discover in the space of an instant that nudity was a cause for self-consciousness.

She was standing at her living-room window by the time Brent had finished dressing and joined her. She had rubbed her hands repeatedly over her arms to bring warmth to her chilled flesh, then had finally clasped her elbows for support. She was oblivious to Brent's approach, until she felt the warmth of his hands through the sleeves of her robe.

"Don't turn away from me, honey. For God's sake, Joy, I . . ."

She resisted the gentle pull of his hands. She didn't want his comfort, when she deserved only his contempt. She had prided herself on her maturity and yet had behaved as selfishly as a child. By tempting him beyond his control, she had used her knowledge of his love for her to gain what she had wanted. But now she could no longer see the future she had always taken for granted. Brent had perceived her feelings about his work far better than she had herself. Because she had always cringed mentally from the dangers he faced, she had disassociated him from his career. She winced inwardly, remembering how she had so often envisioned Brent as her husband, coming home in the evening, from some nebulous occupation, to draw her into his arms.

But it wouldn't be that way, and she sucked in her breath at the realization. There would be lengthy separations, and worry, and constant fear for his safety. With startling insight gained by their shared intimacy, she now saw their lovemaking as a commitment to the kind of life she had never equipped herself for mentally, and suddenly understood that this was just what he had wanted to prevent from happening. She bit her lip, tears of remorse welling in her eyes. She hadn't thought long enough past her passionate need to belong to him to face the responsibility inherent in becoming his lover. She had been the one at fault.

"I'm so sorry, Brent," she whispered, shutting her eyes to hold back her tears.

"Don't do this. . . ." His groaned admonition was muffled against the top of her head as he pulled her back against him. "We have to talk. I need to know what you're thinking, what you're feeling. Once before, I used silence to hide behind, but not this time, Joy. I love you, and mixed with that loving is a wanting that's burning me alive. Don't make me suffer shame for the way I feel, honey . . . please!"

"I'm the one who's ashamed!"

He crossed his arms over hers, and his breath feathered her temple as he spoke. "Maybe it was too soon for us, but what happened in that bedroom felt so right, babe. It was like waking from a nightmare, to find myself safe in your arms."

His grip tightened. "You weren't the only one who fantasized our lovemaking, you know. Many nights I fell asleep thinking of home, and those thoughts always led to you. My mental ramblings began innocently enough, with my missing you, wanting you close. But in the morning I'd find myself aroused, my arms reaching out to make love to you as I had in my dreams.

"Self-hate is a powerful force, Joy. It can destroy the strongest man, and I'm far from that where you're concerned. I had managed to convince myself that all I needed was the physical release of sex." He groaned, his mouth moving against the hollow beneath her ear. "Now I realize that it was always you there in my mind, in my heart. Don't make me hate myself for wanting to love you."

She gasped, and spun around in his arms. Her hands reached up to lock behind the back of his neck. "Is that what you think—that I'm blaming you for making love to me?"

"What else am I supposed to think?" he muttered, his eyes filled with doubt. "When you opened your body as well as your heart to me, it was with trust, and I wanted you so badly I—"

She twisted away from him and hurried across the room with more haste than sense. She stumbled into the coffee table and with a groan dropped to the couch. Her tears broke free at last, and ran in rivulets down her cheeks as she absently rubbed her bruised flesh.

"Oh, God!" she finally said, pressing her fingers against her throbbing temples. "When will you see me as I really am, and not as some beloved fantasy your imagination has conjured up?"

She sighed and shook her head. "I haven't been a trusting child for a very long time, Brent. I'm a woman, and I wanted you to make love to me. That was the only real commitment I made to the future, and that's why I'm ashamed. You're strong, and more than capable of sorting out your priorities. But I'm not even sure what mine are. I have no way of knowing if I possess the strength and dedication you need in a woman. I'd be lying to both of us if I tried to say otherwise."

She heard his muffled tread against the carpet and lifted her head to look searchingly at his face. "All I'm certain of is my love for you," she whispered.

He sat down beside her and placed his hand

over hers until the restless movements of her fingers were stilled. "Let's just take each day as it comes, Joy."

At the intensity of emotion in his voice her eyes widened, and the tenderness in his gaze calmed her emotions as nothing else could have. She nodded slowly, a shaky smile curving her mouth. "You haven't given up on me?"

His fingers tightened, and he stared at her intently. "No matter what happens in the future, I'll always treasure what you've given me."

She leaned against him, and his arms surrounded her with the warm reassurance she so desperately needed. "I only want to be with you, Brent," she cried, pressing her face to his shoulder. "I need that more than I can find words to express."

"Hey, I'm not planning on going anywhere for a while," he teased, tilting her head back with a finger beneath her chin. "I'm not giving you up without a fight."

She couldn't summon a smile, her gaze instead clinging to the glint of determination in his eyes. "Are you sure I'm worth it?"

His head lowered, and his mouth molded itself to hers. His kiss was a bond, a gentle promise to which she responded with every particle of her being. Their lips clung, and parted, only to merge together in a resurgence of passion neither of them found the strength to deny. There was quiet desperation in the arms that struggled to merge their bodies together, but there was also restraint. With a gasp Brent tore his mouth from hers, his eyes blazing with conviction. "Your love is worth everything, Joy," he swore. "Everything!"

Six

Joy couldn't believe the amount of work she'd managed to wade through during the past couple of weeks. She could see the blotter covering her desk again, and a satisfied smile curved her lips as she patted the green paper in triumph. Looking up, she saw the amusement on Grace's face and flushed.

"Pretty cocky, aren't you?"

Joy laughed. "That about describes it," she admitted, once again surveying the top of her desk. "Aren't you proud of yourself?"

"Humph. You're the one who worked like a demon."

"Yes, but I had more than a little help from my friend. It's not every boss who will tell an employee she's blowing it one day, and the next roll up her sleeves and wade into the mess with fists flying. Did I ever thank you properly?"

Embarrassed, Grace got to her feet. Her battered patent-leather handbag dangled from her arm as she waved her hand in a dismissive gesture.

"Don't go getting maudlin on me, girl," she snapped, her mouth as pinched as if she had just sucked on a lemon. "I'll see you on Monday."

Joy's smile widened into a grin as she fondly watched the other woman leave the office. Whenever Grace was carrying that disreputable bag, anyone could tell that she was either coming to work or leaving. In every other respect she was the epitome of the well-dressed businesswoman, from the top of her sleekly groomed salt-and-pepper hair to the toes of her stylish pumps. The rest of the day her poor old purse was relegated to the bottom drawer of her desk, thus preserving her image.

Once, in a confiding mood, Grace had admitted to Joy that she had a superstitious attachment to the battered old thing. Although she had had trouble keeping a straight face, Joy hadn't laughed at Grace's little peculiarity. From that day on she had become her superior's unofficial protégée. Sometimes Joy couldn't help speculating on which one of them was the most ambitious for her to advance in the company, herself or Grace.

Remembering how Grace had hinted that Joy would be offered the position of private secretary to the head of their new Los Angeles branch, she suspected it was the latter. She knew Mr. Welles valued Grace's opinion and had realized that Grace's apparently casual reference cloaked an underlying certainty.

Joy had been both excited and apprehensive at the possibility of a promotion. Any move like that would affect her future, and the future was one thing Joy was not anxious to consider.

She had discussed the possible promotion with Brent, hoping he would understand her reluctance to accept the position if it was offered to her. But he hadn't understood. Instead he had grown curiously silent and uncommunicative and insisted that the decision was hers alone to make. His seemingly callous attitude had precipitated an argument that even now was painful to remember.

The argument had ended in much the same way as the few others they had had. She had tried to make light of the incident and distract Brent from indulging in any serious discussion of their future. She didn't want to know when Brent would be leaving, how long he'd be gone. She didn't want to have to deal with his career yet. And Brent seemed reluctant to pressure her, but she sensed that he was becoming impatient with her indecisive attitude.

With a sigh she pushed the troublesome thoughts from her mind. Stretching her arms high over her head, she leaned back in her chair. She could almost feel the sunlight filtering through the walls of the inner office, and she wriggled with the pent-up energy that was becoming as familiar to her as breathing. She knew its source only too well. Heat filtered through her veins whenever she thought of Brent. Since the night they'd made love he had spent every available moment with her, but it was never enough. He was teasingly affectionate, but always in control of the passion that could so quickly erupt between them.

At first she had taken each day as it came and made herself act with the undemanding affection he wanted. She shivered, aware that it was becoming impossible to keep her longing for him suppressed. She was beginning to resent his control, and increasingly, of late, she had done everything she could to break it. She was playing with fire, but she couldn't hide her need to be in his arms. She hadn't been able to turn her emotions off at will, and she knew Brent wasn't faring much better. The tension between them was building steadily, leaving both of them aching with frustration and unappeased desire.

She wanted him so badly it was almost painful to be apart from him. She had always imagined love to be one of the gentler emotions, not the seething cauldron of sensations that flowed through her blood with the effervescent intoxication of champagne. She expelled her breath slowly while relaxing in her chair. Just being in the same room with him was enough to make her pliant with longing.

So what was she doing, she thought wryly, sitting here brooding when she could be with him? A surge of adrenaline pulsed through her veins as she locked the office, and hurried to collect her car. They were going to a fondue restaurant in Old Town for dinner, but she had just enough time to stop by her parents' house now to say hello before she went home to change.

Automatically tipping Denny when he brought her car around, she was too distracted by a rising sense of anticipation to notice her skirt had inched up her thigh when she climbed into the car. A loud whistle jerked her from her thoughts, and she turned to catch Denny's appreciative leer. She flushed, but by the time she had pulled out into the commuter traffic she was chuckling, her spirits lifting at being the recipient of such blatant masculine attention.

"Anybody home?"

The sound of her voice echoed eerily down the hall of her parents' home, and she winced as the screen door slammed shut behind her.

"Well, look who's here," Brent drawled, appearing from the direction of the den. His voice betrayed his pleasure, and with a breathless laugh she accepted the invitation of his open arms.

"I thought I'd stop by to see you before going to my apartment to shower and change," she explained, her eyes dancing up at him. "Just don't let it give you a swelled head, fella!"

His mouth moved slowly against hers as he whispered a response that tinted the natural rosiness of her cheeks a darker hue. With smiling complacency she linked her hands behind his neck and deepened his kiss. Brent trembled, and drew her closer. What had begun as a teasing caress quickly gained momentum, threatening to engulf them both in the passion that was never far below the surface of their consciousness.

"Brent, why are you . . .?"

Brent stiffened at her father's voice, although his arms remained locked into position around Joy's waist. Slowly Brent lifted his head, his eyes disturbed as he glanced across the hall at the older man. For a heart-stopping moment Joy's flustered gaze moved from one man to the other, trying in vain to decipher their closed expressions. Becoming uncomfortable as the silence lengthened, Joy squirmed, but Brent's clasp only tightened. Confused, she sent her father a pleading glance.

But John never diverted his attention from Brent. "Am I interpreting this correctly, son?" he asked, his face worried.

Turning, but keeping one arm around Joy's waist, Brent nodded. "We love each other, Dad."

The soft drawl held such a tender inflection, Joy could feel tears surging into her eyes. Tilting her head until she was looking up at Brent, she knew her own face matched the love that was reflected back at her from his eyes. Her breath caught as their smiles became a joined promise, and together they returned their attention to the man who was closely observing them.

John looked momentarily stunned by their united front; then a wry smile curved his mouth. The vague air of disapproval he had directed at them vanished as he shook his head ruefully. "I don't know why I'm playing the heavy father," he admitted. "You were pretty up front with your feelings for Joy before you left home. But, son, although she's old enough now to make her own decisions, the problems we discussed then still exist. Concessions and sacrifices are going to have to be made by both of you, and I can't help but worry. I just want you two to be very sure your love can stand up to the pressures you'll have to face together."

Joy gasped. "Dad, you never discussed any of this with me!"

John lifted his hand and motioned them to follow him into the living room. Joy moved forward, in a daze, her eyes never leaving her father's rigid back. She started to question him, but the expression on Brent's face silenced her. With a slight shake of his head he pulled her down beside him on the couch. She complied, but pressed her lips together in frustration. With barely concealed impatience she waited for her father's explanation, her hands clasped so tightly together that her fingers began to ache.

With an air of tiredness John leaned back in an armchair, his elbows on the padded arms and his steepled fingers forming a focal point for his eyes. "You should never have tried putting anything over on your old man," he said, looking at Joy. "You were a naive but precocious young woman four years ago, and it wasn't difficult for me to see you were doing your damndest to drive Brent up a wall backward."

John sighed and shook his head. "Don't blame him for turning to me, Joy. He knew it would be difficult for me to be objective, but I've always been proud that he valued my advice."

"You sent him away?"

Her low tones were accusatory, but Brent stopped her before her anger could erupt. "No, Joy! It was my decision to leave, and mine alone."

"Have I missed something?" Bessie asked, erupting into the room with her usual energy before plopping down on the arm of her husband's chair.

"I'm lecturing our offspring, woman," John said in an attempt to lighten the atmosphere. He slanted his wife a fond glance. "Don't interrupt."

"Just what are you up to, John Barton?"

"Humph. You should ask them that question!"

Obligingly lifting her head, she squinted myopically across the room. "All right, what are you two up to?"

Joy swallowed hard and looked wildly in Brent's direction. But before either of them could utter a word, John drawled, "I caught them trying to set the hall on fire."

"Dad!" Joy's chagrined gasp reverberated around the room.

Bessie's twinkling eyes quickly interpreted the flush on her daughter's cheeks. "How many times did I warn you never to play with matches, Joy?"

"It wasn't matches she was playing with," John explained, covering his betraying grin with the back of his hand.

With a strangled groan Joy lifted her gaze to Brent's face, and exclaimed angrily when she noticed his lips twitching with amusement. "Why, you're right in the middle of this, you beast!"

He smiled and pulled her against his side. "Dad just blew my cover, Mother."

"It was more of a conspiracy," Joy muttered, drawing a shaky breath. "I'm trying to understand why my own parents kept your reasons for leaving home a secret from me. I must have acted like an idiot, since they couldn't trust me with the truth."

"I know how much you blamed yourself for Brent's decision to leave, Joy," Bessie said gently. "We wanted to talk to you, but it wasn't our place to interfere. Brent wanted to give you time to grow up without tying yourself to a commitment, and we had to respect his wishes."

"It's a wonder I managed to grow up at all, with everyone so determined to save me from myself," Joy said resentfully.

"Brent made the only decision possible at the time," John insisted. "Don't blame him for loving you enough to deny himself, and don't view your mother and me as your enemies. We were separated from our son, Joy. You weren't the only one to suffer."

Dropping her gaze, she mumbled, "I do sound rather like a child who's been made to wait four years for a promised treat, don't I?"

Brent's mouth feathered her temple. "Is that all I am to you, a piece of candy?"

Bessie laughed aloud, and John said, "I hope she's over her sweet tooth, son. Some of the places you'll be taking her won't have much of a supply of candy available."

The muscles in Brent's arms contracted at her father's teasing gibe. With a slight hesitation Brent changed the subject, but as he chatted with her parents, Joy's uneasiness increased. Brent was avoiding her eyes, and it wasn't difficult to sense his withdrawal. She was glad her parents were oblivious to the undercurrents filtering between her and Brent, and felt suddenly stifled by a sense of insecurity. She couldn't go on this way much longer, with her own doubts for the future fanned by Brent's negative attitude.

Even after they returned to her apartment, Joy driving her own car and Brent driving the one he'd rented, Joy's depression lingered, and it increased her determination to bring everything out into the open. With this resolution firmly entrenched in her thoughts, much of her tension disappeared beneath the pounding spray of a hot shower. She combed her freshly washed hair and left it to dry naturally into the riotous curls Brent preferred. Hurrying from the bathroom to her bedroom with only her glowing skin for adornment, she caught sight of her reflection and chuckled. She didn't have to guess how Brent would take her habit of trailing around the house as naked as the day she was born!

The staccato rap of knuckles against her bedroom door caused her to jump guiltily, all too aware of the embarrassment she would have felt if Brent had pushed open the door and caught her staring at herself in the mirror. With a muffled groan she searched frantically in her closet for her robe. It took several moments of fruitless searching and another impatient knock at her door before she remembered throwing it in the hamper to be washed. This time she muttered a word her mother had never taught her, as she grabbed the nearest garment and thrust her arms into the sleeves.

It was an old shirt of her brother's she had taken from his room a year ago. Keith, with his lawyer's bent for organization, had always kept a few casual clothes at their parents' home for the times he visited, and she knew he wouldn't miss one measly shirt. She and Shirley had been on an apartment-decorating rampage at the time, and Joy had needed something she wasn't afraid to ruin. She had planned to return the shirt, but a few tiny flecks of gold paint had stubbornly refused to detach themselves from the blue-green plaid. When Keith's next visit passed without his mentioning the missing shirt, she'd come to the conclusion that although confession might be better for her soul, discretion was a heck of a lot smarter.

"I'm coming, I'm coming, for heaven's sake!" she called when Brent rapped on the door again.

She was trying to button the soft flannel and still muttering beneath her breath when she threw open the door. With a flick of her fingers she fastened the gap at mid-thigh and threw up her head in breathless triumph. She was disturbed by the gleam in Brent's eyes, uncomfortable when his gaze slid over her with the ease of a knife slicing through warm butter. But his perusal was almost clinical in its brevity. He was again retreating from her mentally, and she suddenly felt the need to taunt him out of his pose of indifference.

"I couldn't find my robe, but this does just as well, don't you think?" she said in a husky voice.

When she moved her hand in a provocative sweep down her body, he unwillingly responded to the challenge in her gaze. His face reflected his awareness of her deliberate dare, and his understanding of her motives left her feeling foolish. He had the advantage of experience, while she was guided by instinct alone. This unpalatable certainty sapped her confidence as nothing else could. All at once she wanted to hide herself as he leaned against the door and thoroughly inspected her bare thighs.

Her behavior wasn't making anything easy for him, she realized. He was probably furious with her idiotic attempts to seduce him, as he had every right to be. He wanted her as much as she wanted him, and it wasn't fair continually to make him fight himself as well as her. Disgusted by her childish behavior, she backed away.

"I—I'm running a little late," she whispered. "I'll be ready in a minute. Y—you might like that magazine over there. It's one of those fix-it things." She motioned vaguely in the direction of the coffee table in the living room.

"I—I'm fond of fixing things," she added foolishly. She was babbling, but couldn't seem to stop herself.

"Come here, woman!"

At the husky invitation in his voice, she almost crumpled with relief. Turning her head, she saw the tenderness of amused understanding in his eyes. She was already poised for flight, so it took merely a moment to throw herself into his arms. His mouth fitted itself to hers with a hunger she shared, and she could only cling to his neck while the floor rocked beneath her feet.

"What do you have on under that thing?"

Her breath warmed his throat as she laughed. "What do you think?"

His growl vibrated against her lips. "That's what I was afraid of. You could tempt a saint, you know?"

"And you're certainly no saint!"

"Just in case you're in doubt," he muttered, his white teeth gleaming as he smiled, "I'll prove it to you."

Before she could guess his intention, he crouched at her feet. She shivered in delighted surprise when his big hands covered the warm, scented skin of her thighs, his palms curving and flattening. She caught her breath as his fingers traced delicate patterns, then expelled it in a whoosh when his touch slid around the backs of her knees. Well, she thought inanely, she finally knew whether or not he was a thigh man!

But that wasn't all he liked, she realized, her body tensing as his hands slid over the softness of her buttocks. Her flesh was gently kneaded in his hands, until she couldn't tolerate the insecurity of her trembling legs for one second longer. Closing her eyes, she fell forward, her hands burying themselves in his hair as he pressed his face against her stomach.

"Brent . . . please!"

"A saint I'm not," he said hoarsely, rising stiffly to his feet and enfolding her in his embrace. "And that's the trouble. You're driving me crazy, lady, do you know that?"

She closed her eyes and smiled as she leaned against his body. "I don't want to be a lady!"

Her hands fumbled between them, searching for the buttons on his shirt. With a rumble of laughter he caught her hands, effectively stopping her determined movements.

"Oh, no, you don't. I could hear that tummy of yours growling a minute ago."

He chuckled at the disgruntled expression on her face and kissed the tip of her nose. He seemed as reluctant to release her as she was to have him let her go when he turned her around and swatted her on the rear. "Get dressed, so we can go and appease that appetite of yours."

She stepped forward, then glanced at him over her shoulder. Her confidence in herself restored, pure mischief glinted in her eyes as she stretched her arms over her head until the hem of her shirt brushed against the area he had so recently fondled. She yawned languidly. "Since you're so concerned for my well-being, I've developed another appetite you might be able to satisfy." Her lashes lowered in provocative teasing. "Come with me, and I'll tell you all about it."

His eyes twinkled with appreciation at the tart rejoinder, but in their depths was also a delicious promise of retribution. "Since we're both craving the same feast, I already have a good idea of what's on the menu." He paused, a sensual curve to his mouth. "I've spent weeks planning the appetizers, babe. When the time comes, I promise you won't go away hungry."

"It's a good thing I never thought of you as a saint, Brent Tyler," she muttered, lowering her arms with more speed than grace from their frozen position over her head. "You're pure devil!"

He assumed an infuriating expression of innocence that made her want to hit him. "How can you say that, when I intend to fill you with the food of the gods?"

"I . . . you . . . oh . . . !" She slammed the door in his face, but couldn't shut out the sounds of his hilarious laughter. With jerky, uncoordinated movements she began to dress. One up on you, you maddening, egotistical, conceited . . . darling, she thought. Quietly, praying he wouldn't hear, she began to laugh. . . .

By the time they were seated in Brent's car, Joy's good humor was fully restored. A sigh of contentment filtered through her lips, and she snuggled closer against Brent's side. Glancing out the window, she saw the home of the state Capitol lighting the darkness like a beacon. She never passed the building without marveling at its imposing construction as it rose upward from the trees of the park surrounding it. As usual, there was a multi-tiered scaffolding surrounding the rounded structure, where once again repairs were being made on the outer surface.

Joy loved Sacramento, the thriving city it had become as well as the aura of the past that it retained. There was all the excitement of night life to be enjoyed, and yet the quiet, tree-lined streets in some of the older residential areas were relatively unchanged. California's capital managed to thrive in the modern, upbeat world but still kept much of the grace and charm of its early history. The thought made her pause before she turned eagerly toward Brent.

"Let's go to the Crocker Art Museum tomorrow!"

He groaned, slanting her a look of resignation before returning his attention to the road. "I wondered how long it would be before you reverted to childhood."

She giggled and squeezed even closer to his warmth. "Don't be like that, Brent. You know how much I love that old place."

"Don't I just," he mumbled, shaking his head. "You used to drag me around those hallowed rooms often enough."

"Then, you'll take me?"

"I didn't say that."

"Just think of those deliciously cool, mosaic-tiled corridors."

"I'm thinking of my burning feet," he grumbled.

She sat back in her seat with a satisfied smile as Brent placed his arm around her shoulders and cuddled her more comfortably against him. She knew he thought she was crazy to find browsing through a museum entertaining, but she had always been fascinated by antiques. The building housing the museum was immense, so Brent's pained reference to his feet held some validity.

"Now, what devious torture are you planning for me tomorrow?" he asked.

"Do you remember the statue of Joseph and the Holy Child at the entrance of the European exhibit?"

His voice held a teasing inflection. "Vaguely."

"Oh, you're hopeless!"

"Why don't you jog my memory, honey," he whispered, the corner of his mouth twitching. "And while you're about it, just keep pressing against me like that."

She wasn't going to give him the satisfaction of thinking he could disconcert her . . . not after the fiasco earlier this evening. With a slight twist from the waist she allowed his arm to cushion the weight of her breasts, delighted by the success of her maneuver when he drew a sharp breath. She smiled smugly as she reclined against the leather upholstery of the seat. Now it was his turn to sweat a little, she thought. The fact that she wasn't wearing a bra hadn't escaped his notice, and judging by the tightness of his jaw his imagination was working overtime!

He would see the statue soon enough, she decided. With a glimmer of revenge in her heart, she visualized keeping him staring at the lovely thing until his feet smoked. It was sixteenth-century Spanish, of polychromed wood, and beautifully preserved. After centuries the colors—burgundy, gold, brown, and black—were still easily discernible.

She was so lost in the deviousness of her plans, she didn't even notice when Brent turned the car into the parking lot beneath the freeway overpass. As they walked away from the car, she couldn't help being flattered by the blatantly appreciative look the parking attendant sent her.

"Do those pants have to curve quite so snugly around that tight little fanny of yours?" Brent grumbled, sending a dark glance over his shoulder at the grinning attendant.

"Strange," she drawled, amusement deepening her voice, "not so long ago I got the impression you liked that particular area. My imagination must be working overtime."

Walking from the car park to the ten-block section of Old Sacramento was like stepping backward in time. The only jarring note that dispelled the illusion was the tourists, she and Brent included, whose modern garb hardly fit the decor. As their footsteps echoed hollowly on the raised wooden sidewalks, Brent kept a firm grip on Joy's arm, knowing from past experience her propensity for dawdling in the intriguingly decorated shops.

The restaurant they had chosen was one of their favorites. Originally housing the only Sacramento newspaper still in existence, the huge barnlike building had been cleverly reconstructed. Long circular pipes crisscrossed the ceiling, an old press engine turned the pipes, and attached to them on short wooden handles were circular fans. Once used to cool the hot presses, they had been ingeniously renovated to cater to the comfort of the diners.

A congenial waiter with a bristly moustache led them to their table. As they climbed the worn wooden steps leading to an intimate alcove that afforded them a view of the entire restaurant, Joy noticed the surreptitious glances many of the women sent in Brent's direction. In a cream-and-gold sport shirt that stretched across his muscular torso, and brown cords that showed his lean hips and the length of his legs to such advantage, he was quite an eyeful.

"Why do you look like a kitten lapping cream?" Brent murmured after the waiter departed. He had left them a wine list, and now two suspiciously bright blue eyes were studying Joy over its edge.

She lowered her lashes and ran her finger around the rim of her water glass. A tiny dimple beside her mouth punctuated her widening grin as she peeked up at him.

"Those women at that table over there," she

said, nodding in the direction of the central dining area, below, "were eating you with their eyes."

One black brow quirked up, while his mouth curved sensually. "Oddly enough, I've been so busy eating you with my eyes I didn't notice."

She felt the warmth surge in her cheeks, but refused to allow herself to become flustered. Deliberately trailing the tip of her tongue across her lips, she dropped her gaze to his mouth.

"Is that all you'd like to do?"

Her sensual whisper had the desired effect. He leaned forward, his eyes leaping with a hunger he didn't even try to hide. "You're really asking for it, you little tease!"

His gaze moved from her face to linger briefly at the pulse beating out of control against the smooth skin of her throat. Her breathing accelerated in instant response, her breasts rising and falling with a rapidity that was, in itself, embarrassing. The silk of her shirt brushed her rigid nipples, reminding her all too forcefully of the bra she'd left stuffed in her dresser drawer.

As her color deepened, Brent, not content with so slight a victory, allowed his glance to stray even lower, to where her lacy white blouse parted in a deep V.

"You know damn well what I'd like to do to you," he muttered, his voice hoarse.

"Oh, darling." She groaned, her eyes closing as her body shook in response to his words. "I'm not teasing, and neither are you. This is driving us both crazy!"

She didn't know who was more surprised by the abrupt seriousness in her voice, herself or Brent. For long minutes neither spoke, until she broke the silence by blurting, "We can't go on like this, Brent. I want to be with you; to wake up in the morning with your arms around me."

He sighed. "Damn it, Joy. You couldn't want it as much as I do!"

Excited by the swiftness of his capitulation, she reached across the table, her eyes shining. He was fiddling distractedly with his fork, his eyes following the movements of his fingers. But at her spontaneous gesture he dropped the cutlery, and held her hand inside the warmth of his own.

"Oh, Brent," she said, laughter bubbling from her throat. "I've ached with the need to have you make love to me again."

His fingers tightened almost painfully, and her features twisted in bewilderment at the suddenly distant expression on his face. "Don't you think I know that? But I'm the man who awakened that desire in you, and I won't exploit it to hold you. I don't want to add taking you as a sometime mistress to my list of sins, and you don't seem willing to commit yourself to anything more."

Her hands tightly gripped the edge of the table. "I don't know what you expect from me, Brent. I've never asked you to choose between me and your career, but that's the impression you give. I'm only asking for you to love me."

"I just want what's best for you, honey," he muttered, running a shaking hand through his hair as he broodingly inspected her dejected features. "Dad was right, you know. I've learned to do without a great deal of sweetness in my life, and it isn't always easy. There have been times when I've been actively miserable, but there was a job to be done and I did it. But since you're not motivated by the same dedication, it would be harder for you in every respect."

She tilted her chin defiantly, her eyes glittering with purpose. "I want you, not a place on your staff!"

"I know, honey, I know." He rubbed his hand over his eyes. "Oh, God." he groaned. "I want you so badly it's like a burning fire in my middle, but I have to be sure," he whispered. "I have to be sure!"

Tenderness stole her anger as she heard the hopelessness in his voice. "I'm sorry," she murmured, reaching for the strong hand that lay clenched beside his glass. "I know I'm being bitchy, but I can't seem to think clearly anymore. I don't like my indecisiveness any more than you do. You know I've always had a low patience threshold," she added with assumed lightness.

Relief flickered in his eyes. "Don't remind me," he teased, turning his palm upward to grip her fingers with reassuring firmness.

Quickly she channeled their conversation into a lighter vein, knowing she was again avoiding even thinking about a permanent commitment. But she just couldn't give Brent the reassurance he needed. She would be lying if she tried to convince him she could cope with the stress of his career. He had had years to adapt, and she couldn't help thinking he was being stubbornly unreasonable in expecting all the change to come from her. Where were his sacrifices? she thought resentfully. Their glances met, and she had to force herself not to question him. She was being ridiculous, she thought. Surely she had imagined the glimpse of hopeless resignation in his eyes. Of course she had!

Seven

Although Brent had tried to salvage the evening, by the time it drew to a close he had become quiet and withdrawn. When they returned to her apartment he seemed anxious to get away from her, and it was the abruptness of his departure that lingered on in Joy's mind. The long hours of the night were a misery of restless tossing and tumbled sheets. Leaving her bed earlier than usual, she showered and dressed and tried to fill the hours until Brent's arrival. But no matter how busy she kept herself, she never quite managed to shake off the uneasiness she had felt the night before.

He was to come for her at nine, and as the hands of the clock reached and passed the hour Joy was ready to jump out of her skin. Glancing around the freshly vacuumed and dusted apartment, she felt as though the walls were closing in on her. When the shrill ringing of the phone startled her out of her preoccupation, she practically sprinted across the carpet to reach the receiver.

"Brent?"

"Now, why would you suspect that gorgeous hunk is at my place?"

"Oh, hello, Shirley."

Joy felt sick with disappointment. Her voice must have reflected the raw state of her emotions, because Shirley's cheerful tones did an abrupt reversal.

"What's wrong, Joy?"

"Nothing," she replied despondently. "Brent and I are supposed to spend today together, and I've been waiting for him to call."

"You two haven't had a little disagreement, have you?"

Joy hesitated, trying to control her irritation. She didn't want to take out her feelings on her friend, but she certainly wasn't in the mood to stop and chat.

"Nothing like that!" She clenched her teeth, thinking Brent might be trying to reach her at this very minute. "Look, Shirley. Do you think we could talk later? I don't want to tie up the line for too long."

"Boy, do I know what you're going through! Sometimes I think I spend half my life waiting for Carl to call."

"Thanks, Shirl. I'll get back to you."

"Joy!" Shirley's voice squealed over the wire.

With a grimace, Joy eased the phone farther from her ear. She laughed, half with amusement and half with exasperation.

"You almost deafened me, you idiot!"

"All in good cause, my dear." Shirley chuckled. "I called to tell you the Tempests are back in town. There'll be one heck of a party going on tonight at the Holiday Inn across from Old Sacramento, and I thought you and Brent might like to go with Carl and me."

"I don't know, Shirley. . . ."

Joy's voice drifted, and with good cause. The Tempests were an up-and-coming punk rock group; their lead guitarist was a friend of Carl's. Shirley's boyfriend was a quiet, unassuming kind of guy, and Joy was very fond of him. She couldn't say quite the same for his friends, although she supposed they were harmless enough.

The last time the group had descended on Sacramento, it had occupied the entire tenth floor of the high-rise hotel, and at the time Joy had suspected the management would never get over it. She'd left the party at about one, exhausted from the noise, nauseated by the steady flow of liquor, and disgusted with trying to discourage pursuit by the group's drummer. According to Shirley, the festivities had continued through breakfast. Somehow Joy had the distinct impression that a party with the Tempests wouldn't be at all to Brent's liking. She'd already had his reaction to one party. She certainly didn't need another!

"Well, what do you say?" Shirley sounded resigned. "Would you and Brent like to come?"

"Ah," Joy hedged, "how about if I call you back?"

Shirley sighed. "I know what that means," she muttered. "Looks like old Carl will be stuck with just me for company."

"He'll love it!"

"There you go, Joy. You've already made up your mind not to come," Shirley complained. "But I'm not letting you off so easily. You said you'd call, so see that you do!"

"Shirley, you know I—"

"Don't like parties," Shirley mimicked. "The least you can do is ask Brent," she insisted stubbornly. "He struck me as the kind of guy who's used to a little excitement in his life. Not like someone else I could mention!"

That rankled."All right, all right!"

"Promise?"

"That I'll ask Brent?" Joy sighed, suppressing her irritation. "I promise, but if I don't get off this phone I might never get the chance."

"I get the message." Shirley's voice dripped with satisfaction. " 'Bye, love!"

Replacing the phone in its cradle, Joy got jerkily to her feet and moved around the kitchen in a daze. She felt, as she often did when dealing with her friend, that she'd just been run over by a semi. With one eye on the clock, she popped a slice of bread in the toaster and poured herself a cup of coffee. If her stomach kept churning this way, she wouldn't give a tinker's damn for her chances of surviving the morning without being sick.

As she buttered her toast she wished she hadn't given that stupid promise to Shirley. Now she was committed to asking Brent to a party she had no wish to attend. What she really wanted was to spend the day with him, and later to be alone with him in the intimacy of her apartment. She wanted to talk with him, and—

No, that wasn't what she wanted! Her mouth softened as a strain of sensuality entered her thoughts. What she really wanted, needed, was to be held in his arms. She would undress him and run her hands over every inch of his body. Naked, they would lie on the bed and indulge the hunger they felt for each other. They would—

The forceful sound of a knock shattered her pleasant reveries, and she dropped the forgotten toast onto the counter. Dusting her hands carelessly against her dark blue shorts, she ran to the door. Her feet were bare, and her sleeveless blue-and-white striped blouse was knotted beneath her uptilted breasts, leaving the golden skin of her small waist exposed.

Brent was there, a smile in his eyes as he allowed his gaze to wander from the tips of her polished pink toenails to the top of her dusky curled head.

"I know you dressed for coolness," he drawled, leaning his shoulder against the doorframe. "But with you in that outfit I'm going to be hot as hell!"

Smiling, she lifted her arms straight out from

her sides. Her eyes sparkled with mischief as she turned, her movements slow and unhurried as she gave him the full benefit of her attire. As soon as her back was to him, she peeked at him over her shoulder. She saw his appreciative gaze linger on the rounded flesh cradled by her hipbones, and giggled.

"I think all the heat is in your eyes, darling. Just close them, and you won't have a bit of trouble with your blood pressure."

"Smart ass," he teased.

"You must think so, considering the interest you seem to have in it."

He straightened and took a single step in her direction. Already facing forward, she decided to put her position to good advantage.

"Why are you so late?" she scolded, edging around to the kitchen side of the bar. "I was beginning to think I'd been stood up."

Although her voice held a teasing inflection, she knew Brent wouldn't miss the seriousness in the words. The cushions on her badly sprung couch sank under his weight, but he just stretched his legs out in front of him and rested his head against the back.

"How about waiting until we're at the Delta to talk?" he suggested.

"I thought you were going to take me to the museum."

"It's too nice a day to spend indoors."

"But why the Delta?"

She frowned and eyed him with suspicion.

Brent always went to the river when something troubled him. True, at the moment he seemed to be in a good frame of mind, but she sensed an underlying restlessness.

"Hmmm, I've got bread, cheese, and wine in the car," he murmured cajolingly. "All I need is a woman to share it with."

Her eyes mocked him as she placed her hands on her hips in a militant stance. "Just any woman will do, I suppose?"

His mouth moved in what passed for a grin, but his face was curiously expressionless as he responded automatically to her teasing. "For what I've got in mind, only one woman will do," he whispered.

He succeeded in erasing the worried glint from her large brown eyes, his own face lighting up when she flushed with embarrassment. Studying her heightened color he chuckled and surged to his feet with his energetic abruptness that was so much a part of him. Joy swallowed nervously, marvelling at how simply the sound of his raspy voice could send shivery sensations over every bared inch of her skin.

"Sounds promising," she said.

The huskiness of her own voice was deliberate provocation. She saw his eyes flicker in response, and she smiled with all the wiles of Eve when handing Adam the fruit. "I hope you remembered a blanket."

He cleared his throat. "It's in the car," he muttered, thrusting his hands into the pockets of his jeans. "Get some shoes on those pretty feet, and let's get out of here."

When they were about to walk out the door, Joy suddenly gasped. "Oh, I almost forgot," she said. She slanted Brent a wry smile and quickly told him about the party, grinning when he frowned before she had even finished explaining.

"Do you want to go?" he asked.

She shook her head, her eyes holding a message for him to which he couldn't fail to respond. His mouth softened, his eyes dropping to the parted fullness of her lips. "I can't say I like you going to the kind of parties Shirley seems to favor, but I'll take you if it's what you'd like to do."

"I'd rather come back here, with you."

His body tensed, and suddenly he looked away from the longing in her eyes. "Why don't we go to the party? It might be fun."

"Brent, I want to be alone with you."

He heard the disappointment in her voice and drew her against his chest. "We spend plenty of time alone together. It won't hurt us to share a few hours with friends. Anyway, you don't want to get Shirley mad at me, do you?"

Was he getting bored with her company already? she wondered, lowering her lashes to hide the hurt in her eyes. With a sigh, she shook her head. "I'll call her," she said, pulling away from him to go to the phone.

After she had hung up the receiver, she went to join Brent. He was standing by the pool, his legs wide apart as he stared into its blue depths. The smile on her face faded when she noticed his expression. The skin over his prominent cheekbones seemed to have tightened into brooding harshness. His shoulders were hunched, as if they supported a weight only he could carry. She stumbled in her haste to reach him, but when he turned, his quick grin instantly dispelled the illusion.

"Ready?" he said.

She placed her hand in his. "Can we take my car?"

"That bucket?" he chided in pretended shock. "You expect me to torture my legs in that little thing?"

"It wouldn't be the first time!"

At first she couldn't understand why she wanted to use her car instead of the luxurious vehicle Brent had leased. She had no air conditioning, and the August day was already sweltering. By mid-afternoon the temperature would be similar to a blast furnace. Brent's rental car was sleek and cool, but it was also impersonal. Suddenly she sensed a need for the comfort of familiar surroundings. In her mind, the other vehicle had become inexplicably . . . alien.

"All right, but I'm driving," he conceded, shaking his head. "Help me get the stuff out of the trunk."

They quickly transferred the preparations for their picnic to her car. Slamming the trunk lid closed, Brent eyed her.

"I'm in love with a pack rat," he muttered disgustedly. "I don't know how old some of that junk is, but it looks like it dates back before you were born."

"Well," she replied cheerfully, "we managed to fit everything in, so what are you complaining about?"

"I bet your boss has never inspected your file cabinets," he said, holding open the door while she seated herself. "I know there must be method to your madness, but one look and he'd probably fall at your feet in shock."

As he walked around the car, he was laughing. When he sat beside her, she glared at him. "I'll have you know I'm very organized. Everything in that trunk is a dire necessity!"

His mouth twitched as he turned the key in the ignition. "Even the inflatable life raft?"

"What if I were stranded in the woods and had to sleep on the ground?" Her tone held triumph. "It would make a perfect air mattress."

"Not without a pump to blow it up!"

The engine rattled to life, and she yelled over the noise as he gunned the accelerator to keep it from dying. "Where there's a will, there's a way."

"And you're about the most willful baggage I've ever come across!"

Surprisingly happy with his goading, she sat back in her seat with the remnants of a smile quirking her lips. She noticed Brent's mouth curling in amusement. His thigh touched hers as he twisted, and she sent him a glance of mocking innocence.

"Is something wrong?" she asked politely.

"My God, this thing isn't built for anyone much over five feet tall, that's for sure."

"You know where the lever is. You can move the seat back if you'd like."

"Thank you," he said, sending her a speaking glance. "That's very magnanimous of you."

"I thought so." She quickly averted her face to hide her amusement.

With a grunt, Brent adjusted the seat. Just a single dimple peeped out beside her mouth, caused by his heartfelt sigh of relief. He backed the small silver car out of the parking space.

As they drove, with the windows rolled down to take advantage of the breeze, Joy looked out at the passing terrain. She sighed with pleasure as they approached the Delta area of the Sacramento River. Brent was right, she thought. Today was too beautiful to spend inside. She knew this vast inland sea was a very special place for him, which must be why he'd decided to bring her here to talk. She remembered days long ago that they'd had together; the picnics enjoyed by these tree-shaded banks. They had been happy times, but today would create for her the happiest memory of all, she thought with determination. Glancing at Brent and noticing his air of preoccupied isolation, she shivered with a return of her earlier foreboding.

This time of the year the grass in most places was burnt brown from the hot sun and its high temperatures, but the trees dipping down to the water would provide welcome shade. She hardly waited for Brent to park, before jumping out and surveying their surroundings. She needed to escape from the forced intimacy of the car, and, throwing back her head, she joyously inhaled the scents of the river.

"Come on, little nature lover," Brent called as he lifted the heavy wicker basket containing their lunch out of the trunk. "Put those waving arms to some use and help me spread this on the ground."

Forcing a show of lightheartedness she was far from feeling, she dragged a dilapidated tarp from his hands. "Couldn't you find something a little less . . . ummm . . . used for us to lie on?"

"We will either stand or sit or walk," he muttered, his eyes narrowing in warning. "You can take your choice."

"You're no fun at all!"

They attacked their lunch, but Joy found herself paying more attention to the man seated beside her than to the food. His closeness was creating havoc inside her, and she found herself chewing and swallowing automatically. She was supremely conscious of the muscles beneath his tanned skin, shown to advantage in a sleeveless tank top. They rippled with every movement of his arm, the sheen of perspiration on his body glinting disturbingly. When he pulled the knit shirt off, she could hardly keep herself from groaning aloud.

He lay back with a sigh of satisfaction, and her gaze seemed to be glued to the dark hairs curling on his chest. Her breasts remembered their softness, with evocative results. She gritted her teeth and closed her eyes, only to open them convulsively just seconds later. But this time she saw the blue fire of his gaze on her. Disconcerted, she averted her head and began pulling at a tuft of dry grass.

"Brent?"

His name was soft on her lips, but held so much naked longing she couldn't bring herself to gauge his reaction. She stared out at the muddy waters of the river, grateful for the slight breeze that brushed gently against her heated cheeks. Their little cove was secluded, and the only other sounds of life came from far down the river. The knowledge of their isolation worked on her mind like an aphrodisiac, and she hurriedly fumbled with the front of her blouse. The knot gave way beneath her hands, and she heard Brent's stifled exclamation as she slowly parted the material.

"For God's sake, Joy," he muttered harshly, the deterrent in his voice not matching the intensity of his eyes as they roamed hungrily over her sun-kissed flesh. With a smile of triumph she leaned forward and traced his features with the tip of her finger. He moaned softly when the distended tips of her breasts brushed against his chest. He closed his eyes, and she could feel the repressed tension in his body, his chest heaving as he fought for control. When he lifted his hands Joy was certain he meant to push her away, but, trembling slightly, they began roaming over the warm skin beneath her loosened blouse. Fire streaked through her at his touch, and she could no longer resist the taste of his mouth.

To her delight he responded, his tongue

savoring the delicacy of her lips before plunging deeply. The thrusting duel that arose matched the writhing cadence of the bodies as they struggled to fuse themselves together through their restrictive clothing. With a groan he tore his mouth from hers. His hands spanned her waist, and he positioned her more fully above him.

With her arms braced beside his shoulders she lowered herself until Brent was able to capture a puckered nipple in his mouth. The moist warmth as he gently suckled and teased the responsive bud drove all reason from her mind. The fire moved from her breasts downward, and she rocked her hips against him in an attempt to quench the burning sensation between her thighs.

"Oh, God!"

His cry was anguished as he jolted them both into a sitting position. Stunned, she watched as he angrily tugged his shirt back on. He sat breathing deeply, his arms crossed over his updrawn knees, his head lowered. Left with no alternative she retied her blouse, and sat with her fists clenched in her lap. The audible breath she drew into her lungs was a shaken attempt to gain control, but it sufficed to put an end to the silence stretching between them.

"I'm sorry, honey," he muttered. "I didn't bring you here to make love to you."

"I know that," she murmured, running her hand caressingly over his bent head. "We can't help what happens when we're together."

"This has got to stop, but I—"

She forced a laugh. "I know." She sighed and bent forward to place a kiss against his forehead. "Don't torture yourself, or me, any longer, darling. We've spent the last weeks trying to come to terms with our relationship, but nothing has changed. We love each other, and we should feel no guilt for wanting to express that love. I want you more than ever," she continued dreamily, "and I know you want me just as badly. Stay with me tonight, Brent. It's what we both need, can't you see that?"

"Stop it, Joy!"

He lifted his head, his mouth clamping tightly closed as he observed the shock in her eyes. The muscles in his face worked convulsively, but all she was really aware of was the ravaged expression in his eyes. She suddenly knew what he had to tell her, and that dreadful certainty enclosed her in an icy shell.

"How can I make you understand that I can't make love with you again and just walk away?" he whispered shakily. "These weeks together have strengthened our attraction for each other, but they've accomplished little else. Don't you think I know why you've changed the subject every time I've tried to discuss my work with you? It's something you can't bear to think about, because it would mean facing the reality of our situation. But one of us has to think past the wanting, Joy."

"You could try speaking to me openly, instead of trying to prepare me for disappointment as though I were still a child to be protected."

"All right," he said tiredly. "But you're not going to like what I have to say."

"I've already gathered that," she said, her eyes resolute as they held his gaze.

Brent hesitated, as though searching for words, and rubbed his hands against the knotted muscles of his neck. "Don't look at me like that, Joy. Do you think this is easy for me?"

"I'm sorry if I'm not as much in control as you'd like me to be. I'll try to do a better job of concealing my emotions from now on. After all, I should be able to absorb at least a little of your technique."

He didn't respond to her jibe with anything other than a disgusted snort. "Sarcasm isn't going to solve a damn thing!"

"Then, what will?" she retorted, her features twisting with anger.

He leaped to his feet and strode toward the edge of the bank. "I can see from the mood you're in that there will be no reasoning with you."

"You expect me to be reasonable, when I don't even know what this is all about?"

He turned and shook his head in frustration. "I've spent the better part of the night trying to decide that for myself, but I'm no nearer a solution to our problem."

"What problem?" she practically screamed, rising to her knees and facing him with restrained fury. "The only problem I can see is your opinion of me. I have the right to make decisions regarding my life, but as long as you think me incapable of knowing what I want, we'll never get anywhere. I don't ever want you to walk away from me, but I want a man, not a protector!" She pounded her fist on the ground. "Damn it, Brent! Doesn't what I want matter at all to you?"

He strode over to her and without ceremony pulled her to her feet. "That smacks quite a bit of moral blackmail, my love."

"You know I don't mean anything of the kind," she snapped, biting down on the soft underside of her bottom lip and shaking her head.

"That's the problem," he said gently. "You're too inexperienced to know what you do mean, let alone want. You placed me on a pedestal in your mind, and never gave any other man a chance to get close to you, Joy. Like the greedy bastard I am, I took advantage of your blind devotion, but I've tried my damndest to make it up to you. You've got to try to understand my position."

"Oh, hell." He groaned. "I'm so afraid of hurting you, babe!"

"There has to be give-and-take in any relationship," she insisted stubbornly. "We'll never achieve an understanding of each other if we keep our feelings in limbo. At least I'm woman enough to know I need to express myself."

"Just in bed, or out of it?"

She winced, her eyes widening as the color seeped from her face. His taunt caused her indescribable pain, but she was determined to retain a semblance of dignity. With coolly deliberate movements she withdrew her arm from his clasped fingers and turned toward the car.

His hands closing over her shoulders effectively stopped her. "Oh, God!" he said, pulling her back against his body. "I didn't mean that."

She turned slowly and braced her hands against his chest. "I think you did," she whispered. "I think you meant every word."

She smiled bitterly. "I suppose I should offer you my congratulations! You've been looking for a way out of our relationship, and now you've found it."

His hands tightened; then he slowly released her. "Maybe you're the one looking for a way out," he said, his eyes searching her features. "Is that what this hysteria is all about, Joy?"

His voice held indifference, as though he couldn't care less what answer she gave. Recklessly she retorted, "You're so good at doing my thinking for me, figure it out for yourself."

She saw disgust in his eyes at her childishness, and fought a rising sickness. She was striking out at him with her words and was only succeeding in convincing him of her immaturity. With a sob she retreated and stumbled over the edge of the tarp. Before she could fall she was in his arms, trapped against the warmth of his body.

"Let me go," she pleaded, her head moving restlessly against his chest.

"Joy, please be reasonable," he said, his words muffled against her hair. "I'm only trying to—"

"I know what you're trying to do," she cried,

pushing her tumbled hair from her flushed cheeks with shaking hands.

"All these weeks you've been so patiently controlled," she said derisively. "I thought you wanted to give us time to get to know each other again, but it wasn't that at all. You just didn't want a sexual relationship to force you into making another mistake, did you?"

"What in hell do you mean, another mistake?"

"Now's not the time to be evasive, and don't look at me like that. God, I hate it when you hide behind that icy control of yours."

"I haven't always been controlled," he reminded her grimly. "I remember one night when you held the upper hand."

"You'll never forgive yourself for being human enough to want me, will you? Becoming my lover was something you'd never planned on. Don't you think I know that by now?"

She sighed, and turned to stare sightlessly out at the river. "It was your first mistake, unless you want to count coming home at all. The second was letting your guilt goad you into a feeling of responsibility toward me."

"You know damn well that's not all I feel for you," he said shortly. "I want all the love you have in you to give, but I want it for always, Joy. An affair with me is no solution. Sharing a bed would relieve sexual tension, but neither of us could be happy with that for long. I'm trying to give you freedom of choice, but you're not making it easy for me."

"Just what choice are you giving me?" she questioned bitterly. "You've been leading up to something all day, Brent. What is it?"

"I would do everything possible to make you happy, Joy, but it's going to take me time to work things out."

"How much time?"

A muscle flexed in his jaw, but the eyes that held hers were determined. "Six months, maybe a little longer."

"Just where will you be while you're busy working things out?" she muttered sarcastically.

"Part of the time I'll be overseas on assignment, but—"

She nodded, her glance scathing. "I understand. You've had a nice little diversion, but now you're becoming restless. If you're bored with leading a normal life this quickly, the least you can do is be honest about it."

"I'm not the one weaving romantic daydreams around our relationship," he insisted, his mouth twisting wryly. "If you love me the way you say you do, a little time apart isn't going to change anything. It just might make it easier for you to decide whether or not you want to be tied to me. I'm a possessive man, and what I have I hold. You have to be sure that a life with me is what you want!"

"What if I tell you I'm already sure?" she whispered, lowering her head and staring fixedly at his chest.

"Telling me is one thing," he said, his voice growing harsh. "But can you make me believe it?"

Not content with his view of the top of her head, he tilted her chin up until their eyes met. She was shocked by his words into realizing the extent of her dilemma. Brent *was* certain of what he wanted, and she was too inexperienced to know if she could handle the demands he would make of her if they allowed their relationship to go further. Realizing she was without an answer to his question, she moved away from him, withdrawing mentally as she saw his eyes darken with anguish. His arms dropped to his sides, no longer reaching for her. She felt abandoned and more alone than she'd ever been.

Eight

Joy had suffered pain before in her relationship with Brent, and she had known rejection. But sweet heaven, she thought, nothing had ever prepared her for the grief that was tearing her apart. By the time they reached her apartment she was almost faint with the effort to keep her composure. At her door she turned to face him. "How soon will you be leaving?"

He drew her into his arms and ran a shaking hand through her hair. "I have to wait a couple of days for a flight, but I'll be back as soon as possible. Some time apart is necessary for both of us, Joy. Right now we're on fire for each other, and neither of us is in any condition to look at our situation objectively. All I can think of when I look at you is the way you moan when I touch you, the way your body fits against mine, the taste of your mouth, the warmth of your breast straining against my hand." He pulled back from her slightly. "And you can't honestly claim that your ability to reason is any better than mine."

She sighed deeply and placed her hand tentatively against his chest while his hands tightened around her waist. "You're doing what you think best, Brent, and maybe you're right. I . . . after this afternoon, it's clear we do need some time apart," she whispered tiredly. "Maybe it would be better if we didn't see each other until you return."

"But there's the party tonight," he protested, his flashing eyes rejecting her suggestion. "I want to take you, honey."

"I don't think so." She pulled away from him and stepped inside her apartment. "I never really wanted to go, anyway."

"You've already accepted Shirley's invitation for us both."

"She'll understand."

Quickly, before she could change her mind, she closed the door. She rested her forehead against the wooden surface, silently praying for him to go away. The last glimpse she'd had of his face had told her of the leashed impatience building inside him because of her apathetic attitude, but she was past dissembling. The only way she could discover the strength of her love for him was by letting old dreams die. She had achieved one of her youthful fantasies. She was now a woman Brent wanted badly, but his desire for her was driving them apart. Like her, he had allowed himself to be carried away on the tide of an impossible dream, his conscience somehow justifying the sexual attraction between them. But they both had to go beyond that sexual attraction. She had to grow up and either accept the reality of the man in all his complexities or try to build a life without him. There could be no middle ground.

She sagged heavily against the wall as she listened to his footsteps crunching on the gravel. Her vision was blurred, her legs shaking with the effort it took to walk across the room to the phone. Lifting the receiver, she dialed a number with the careful concentration of a person in shock.

"Shirley?" She heard herself speaking like someone in a dream. "Brent can't make it, but I'd like to go tonight."

She shut out the sound of her friend's voice and blanked out her surroundings by simply closing her eyes. She needed music and laughter. She needed excitement to return life to her deadened emotions.

"If you're sure Carl won't mind my tagging along, I'll meet you at your place at eight."

"We'll have a ball," Shirley enthused. "Wear something sexy!"

Replacing the receiver, Joy automatically retreated to the bedroom. A grim smile curved her mouth. Brent thought she needed the company of other men before she could be sure of her love for him, and maybe he was right. Maybe there would be someone at the party tonight who could make her forget her uncertainties. She needed to find an outlet for her pain. She needed . . . Stumbling, she fell across the bed and clutched the spread with desperate fingers. She needed him! Oh, God! She needed Brent!

Her head throbbed with the music, and she took another swallow of the potent mixture in her glass. When a male hand fastened itself to her arm, she didn't resist. She simply placed her drink on an adjacent coffee table and went with the man.

Her body felt the pulse of the beat, and she automatically twisted in an accommodating movement. Without thought she swayed and danced around the makeshift dance floor with every indication of pleasure. She couldn't remember the name of her partner, but it didn't matter. The eyes that roamed over her figure, which was displayed to advantage in an off-the-shoulder silver sheath, mattered least of all.

She was sexy, she was desirable, and she was having fun. Those were the only important things to remember. In a way it was true, she realized. Thanks to a little liquid refreshment, she was having a blast!

After the dance, her partner led her off the dance floor and got her another drink. She was leaning against the wall, her eyes half closed, when Shirley found her.

"Honey, don't you think you'd better go easy on that stuff?" her friend asked worriedly. Joy looked at the squat glass she was holding and giggled. The man beside her laughed too, and pulled her more closely against him. Looking up, she saw the concern in Shirley's eyes and giggled again.

"It—it's called a Kamakazi Bomber. Want a taste?" she said stupidly.

"Joy, why don't you let us take you home? This really isn't your scene."

"Hey, don't go giving my girl ideas. You want to stay with me, don't you, honey girl?"

Owlishly, Joy tried to focus on the stranger's face. What was his name? Bill? . . . Phil? . . . Oh, well! It didn't matter. He was being so nice to her. She was having a wonderful time, she really was. She said as much to Shirley, and couldn't understand why it made her friend so angry.

"Come on, Joy. I'm getting you out of here!"

Bill—or was it Phil?—merely tightened his hold when Shirley reached for Joy's arm. "I don't think so, lady. You want to stay with me, right, sugar? We're going to make a night of it. Tell your friend to buzz off."

Joy glanced uneasily in his direction. He was really very nice, but just then his voice hadn't been at all pleasant. He was glaring at Shirley, and his face seemed almost menacing. Why was he so angry? She knew Shirl could be irritating at times, but she was a great friend. Hadn't she invited her to this terrific party?

"Come on, Joy," Shirley coaxed, her voice almost desperately eager. "Carl's bringing the car around from the garage."

Swaying, Joy was glad for the warm hand that

supported her hip. Another bubble of laughter broke from her throat as she shook her finger at Shirley.

"Party pooper!"

"That's right, babe," Bill/Phil whispered in her ear.

Joy turned on him. "Don't call me that! Only Brent can c—call me that!"

Had that been her voice? she wondered. Odd, it didn't sound like her. She never slurred her words, and God . . . her head felt as though she'd crawled inside the bass drum.

The hand that steadied her was now rubbing up and down her side from waist to thigh. "Don't let sourpuss, here, get to you, angel. I'll tell you what. Let's you and me head down to my room, and we'll make our own fun without worrying about any interruptions."

Joy scowled and began to struggle in his arms as he half dragged her toward the door. He wasn't nice at all, she thought. If he were, he wouldn't have reminded her of Brent. She didn't want to go anywhere with him. She wanted to be with Brent. Dazedly she gazed around the opulent room. She needed Brent so much. Why wasn't he here?

Velvet draped the sitting-room windows. What looked to her like dozens of frantically happy people were sprawled on every available surface, but she couldn't find Brent. Her fastidious nature was suddenly revolted by the sight of food and drink overflowing the tables and portable bar, and she felt her stomach churn alarmingly. The room was thick with smoke, and her eyes burned like fire. That was the reason for the tears that were running down her cheeks, she assured herself.

"I'm going to be sick!"

As soon as she spoke, she felt the man at her side recoil. His arm was replaced by Shirley's. The transfer was accomplished so swiftly, Joy had little time to decide whether or not she was sorry.

"Let's go to the ladies' room, honey," Shirley said.

Joy mumbled her acceptance, her feet stumbling as she navigated the distance. Shirley opened a bathroom door and guided them both inside. Joy had never felt so awful in her life. She barely had time to reach the toilet before she began retching, while Shirley's soothing voice sounded behind her. A damp towel wiped the beads of sweat from her forehead, and when the spasms finally eased, Shirley gently helped her to stand.

Through it all Joy's tears never stopped flowing, and Shirley's patient ministrations didn't help her establish any control. She leaned against her friend, sobbing hysterically. Her hiccoughing words made little sense, even to herself. She was saying something about Brent and wanting to die . . . but she was so mixed up.

"I want to go home," she finally moaned.

"That's just where we're going," Shirley responded grimly. "We'll leave by the connecting suite. I don't want any more trouble with superstud, out there."

"I'm s—sorry, Shirl," Joy said, leaning her head on the other girl's shoulder as they exited the bathroom. "I—I'm sorry for spoiling your p—party."

"I'm the one who needs her head examined. I never should have brought you here!"

Joy figured she must have slept most of the way home. After reaching the parking lot and practically crawling into the back seat of the car, she couldn't remember anything until she found herself being helped onto the sidewalk by a worried Carl. She must have tripped against the curb, because the next thing she knew he had lifted her into his arms and was quickly heading in the direction of the apartments. She raised her head and smiled at Shirley, who hurried along beside them. When Shirley's expression didn't lighten, Joy forgot all about trying to be cheerful. Tiredly, she rested her head against Carl's shoulder.

"What the hell happened to her?"

Joy's body jumped at the sound of Brent's voice, coming from out of the shadows. When she saw his face, she whimpered his name and reached out to him. As Brent enfolded her in his arms, Carl willingly released his burden. Ignoring Brent's thunderous expression, she burrowed her face in his neck with a relieved cry. She heard Shirley talking and then Carl's voice emphasizing something to Brent, but their words just flowed meaninglessly around her. She was only conscious of the ponderous beat of his heart against her hand and the clean musky scent of the man she loved.

Shirley searched in Joy's purse for her key and opened the door. "Carl, you go on over to my place," she said, turning to place a hand on Carl's arm. "I want to talk to Brent before I leave."

Carl frowned at the leashed fury in Brent's features. "You sure you want to go this alone, honey?"

"I can handle anything Mr. Brent Tyler cares to hand out, and then some," Shirley retorted, tilting her jaw at a determined angle. "But he does deserve more than the sketchy explanation we gave him." She smiled. "I'll only be a few minutes. Just long enough to fix Joy a pot of coffee and say a few words to Brent in her defense."

"You don't have to defend Joy to me." Brent grunted, carrying his burden through the door and striding across the room to the couch.

Shirley simply sucked in her breath in an exasperated hiss and waved good-bye to Carl before closing the door. While Brent settled a groaning Joy as comfortably as possible on the couch and set about preparing a cold compress for her head, Shirley made a full pot of coffee. When the preparations were completed, she walked over to stare down at her friend's pale features.

"You've really come a cropper, haven't you, hon?"

"Oh, Shirl," Joy whimpered, clutching her throbbing head. "I'm so ashamed!"

Brent returned at that moment with the freshly dampened washcloth in his hand. Folding it and placing it over Joy's forehead, his eyes glittered with anger. "You should be!"

"Don't you blame her," Shirley raged, her hands on her hips. "If anyone was to blame, it was me, for not noticing how upset she was!"

"All right." Brent sighed, shaking his head. "Just what did happen at that party tonight?"

"Carl and I tried to get Joy to go easy on the booze, but she wouldn't listen," Shirley began to explain. Joy squawked a protest, but no one took the least notice of her from her sprawled position on the couch. Her so-called friend simply sent her a vaguely shamefaced glance before continuing her catechism.

"After I got her detached from some creep who had been dogging her footsteps most of the evening, we went into the ladies' room."

Shirley's laughter was grim. "I thought we were going to have a real problem with him, but you should have seen his face when Joy said she was going to be sick. It would have been funny if I hadn't been so scared. Carl had gone downstairs to bring the car around from the garage, and the bastard was trying to drag Joy to his room."

Again Joy started to object to Shirley's detailed account of the evening, but Brent silenced her with a glowering glance from beneath half-closed lids.

"I tried to call you at the Bartons'," Shirley confessed. "When Carl and I began to notice the crazy way Joy was acting I thought you might be able to talk some sense into her."

Brent nodded. "I went out for a drive, then came here. When Joy didn't answer her door, I suspected she'd gone to the party with you. I was just ready to put in an appearance, when you drove up."

"At least you care enough to be worried about her!"

Joy moaned at the sarcasm in Shirley's voice and turned her head against the cushion. She wished it was deep enough to bury her whole body inside, but she couldn't have everything! As she had expected, she was once more ignored by the other two.

"Of course I care," Brent was muttering, his eyes narrowing on Shirley's condemning features. "What made you think I didn't?"

Placed firmly on the hot seat, Shirley rose to the occasion quite adequately, describing in detail Joy's miserably revealing conversation as they left the party. But does she have to repeat everything word for word? Joy wondered mutinously. Well, this was certainly one way to sober up quickly. Hearing your innermost feelings discussed as though you were nonexistent went a long way toward wrenching a person from an alcoholic haze.

Wearily Joy lowered her lashes over her burning eyes. Oh, Lord! If that last glimpse she'd had of Shirl's face was anything to go by, the other woman's protective instincts were well and truly aroused. Joy was afraid she knew what was coming, and childishly held her breath as she waited for further developments.

"I know it's none of my business what goes on between you two," Shirley said, "but I can't stand to see Joy hurting so badly that she doesn't give a damn what happens to her. I know from experience that she'll survive the pain, but if the price she pays means having her love for you turn to hate, it's only what you deserve!"

Shirley slammed the door behind her with such force, Joy expected the hinges to fall off on the spot. When the door held she sat up and cradled her aching head in her hands. She didn't hear Brent move, but the next minute a cup of black coffee was being held out to her.

"I don't want it," she protested, her stomach lurching as the aromatic steam tickled her nose.

"Drink it, Joy!"

"I can't, I—"

"You can," he declared imperiously. "You're the one who went out and got sloshed, so you'll have to suffer the cure."

She winced at the impatience in his voice and slowly lifted the steamy beverage to her petulant mouth. She knew there wasn't any use in arguing with him, and she was too exhausted to try. Carefully she finished the drink. She uttered a thankful sigh when the last of the liquid was gone and she could replace the cup on the coffee table.

But her reprieve was short-lived. No sooner had the mug left her shaking hand than she was lifted in hard arms and carried through her bedroom, into the bath. Without uttering a word Brent placed her on her feet, keeping a confining arm around her waist. With his free hand he turned on the shower and adjusted the spray to his satisfaction. Then he turned to her and, ignoring her wriggling resistance, calmly proceeded to strip her to the skin.

Although not completely cold, the water on her heated flesh caused her to shudder. She would have escaped from the punishing torture if she had been able. But to her dismay Brent stood guard by the shower door, his bulk clearly defined through the opaque glass.

She had her hand on the hot-water control but jerked it back at the sound of Brent's voice. "If you try to turn that handle, you'll have company so fast it'll make your head swim."

"At least then I won't be the only one to suffer," she retorted.

Resigned to her fate, Joy began lathering her body and hair. She rinsed thoroughly and was just beginning to enjoy the coolness of the water pounding against her tense muscles when the door opened. Brent's gaze slid over her dripping body, before he swore beneath his breath and turned off the water. He gripped her arm and practically dragged her from the tiled stall.

"This is ridiculous," she gasped as he began to towel her dry. "I'm perfectly capable of—"

"Shut up!"

Brent's snarling command sent her unspoken words spinning from her mind, and she retreated once more into confusion. Like a puppet she allowed herself to be dried, brushed, and, finally, enveloped in her comfortable front-zippered robe. He even smeared gel on her toothbrush and stood over her while she attended to her teeth. With unusual docility she allowed herself to be led to the kitchen table, where another mug of coffee was placed in front of her. She scowled up at him but didn't dare try to initiate a conversation. Just one look at his broodingly harsh face was enough to make her cautious.

But by the time he had topped off her cup for the fifth or sixth time, she was seething with rebellion. She opened her mouth to utter a scathing retort, but she hesitated when he lowered himself into the armchair. Although he gave every indication of indolence as he lounged with his head against the tall back, she sensed a coiled tension inside him that didn't augur well for his temper. She shivered convulsively and suspected that, far from being over, her ordeal had just begun.

Nine

"Have you finished?"

Joy winced at the sound of his voice. Her eyes darted nervously to the unappetizing dark liquid remaining in her cup. Before he had a chance to view the evidence, she crossed the room and guiltily rinsed the remains down the sink. Her relief was enormous as her body obediently responded to her brain's signals, without a sign of the stagger she had half expected. With Brent's eyes following her, she was thankful to be in a condition normal enough to pass inspection. She was as sober as a judge, she thought. She almost ruined the slight advantage she had gained by laughing, but muffled the sound with a cough.

Brent didn't insist on any more liquid restoratives, a decision her sloshing stomach heralded with relief. Her relief lasted all of thirty seconds, though, before new flutterings in her midsection replaced the old as he rose to his feet and joined her. When every nerve ending in her body responded to his presence in the confined area, she decided another cup of coffee might not have been such a bad idea after all.

"I—I appreciate w—what you've done for me, but I—I'll be all right now, Brent."

While she stammered like a fool, she backed as far away from him as possible in the tiny kitchenette. The handle of the refrigerator door pressing painfully against her spine stopped her retreat, but the discomfort was preferable to any contact with Brent's body.

The way his mouth contorted couldn't be called a smile. It was more like a feral grimace, and it emphasized the gleam of anger in his eyes.

"Why, Joy?"

It was the moment of truth, but still she sought to evade an answer. "I don't understand what you mean."

He placed a hand beside her averted head and leaned forward. "Why?"

The rasping softness of his voice was pure intimidation. But she'd be damned if she was going to show the reaction he expected! Anger gave her the courage she needed to withstand his probing. Deliberately meeting his eyes, she shrugged noncommittally.

"I was in the mood for a party."

Her uncaring attitude seemed to break his

barrier of controlled indifference. Grasping her soft upper arms, he pulled her forward and lifted her until her toes barely reached the floor. The heat from his hard frame was as unbearable as the sight of his strained features.

"Were you also in the mood to be raped?" he snarled.

She uttered a scornful exclamation and twisted against his hold. "I know Shirley gave you the impression I was in dire peril, but that's far from the truth. I . . . maybe I wanted to go with him."

His fingers tightened briefly before they eased their pressure on her flesh. His whole body stilled as if in shock. Swallowing nervously, she regretted her deliberately wounding words. But sanity came much too late to do her any good.

"A damned one-night stand," he gritted through clenched teeth. "Is that what you wanted?"

Unadulterated fury swept through her and stripped her of any semblance of dignity. "One night or several, it really doesn't matter anymore, does it? You should know that!"

He inhaled sharply, his features whitening. Hard on the heels of her sarcastic jibe came the uncontrollable need to escape his rapier glance. With a muffled curse she brushed past him and stormed into the living room. How could he, even if her own words condemned her, believe her capable of such behavior? He was the one responsible for her need to dull the pain he had inflicted so easily, and she refused to give him the satisfaction of knowing just how vulnerable he had made her.

Well, let him think what he wanted! As long as he was convinced of the shallowness of her feelings, he was off the hook, wasn't he? If he didn't believe her mature enough to know her own mind, he wouldn't have to invent any more excuses. Why not make it easy for him? Right now, she just didn't give a damn!

Oh, God! That wasn't true . . . could never be true. She did care what he thought of her. She reached the couch and curled up in one corner. Nearly choking, she held back the sobs rising in her throat and wrapped her arms across her chest to subdue the chills wracking her body.

She didn't protest when Brent's weight depressed the cushions beside her huddled form. He began to speak softly, but she didn't want to listen. Her mind was in turmoil at the thought of what she had almost done that night, and her subconscious chose apathy as protection. Emotional exhaustion had taken its toll, and she stared sightlessly down at the carpet. She could derive no meaning from his words . . . no meaning from anything!

"Damn it, Joy! You're tearing me apart!"

He jumped to his feet and strode across the room to the window. He reached into his shirt pocket and withdrew his cigarettes and lighter, but his movements were jerky. He'd be leaving soon, she thought sadly as she watched him. He'd go back to his dangerous world, leaving her behind to worry, to await anxiously the tragic news. How much harder it would be now, after all they had shared. Brent had been right to stop them. . . .

He stood by the window, unnaturally still, his shoulder against the wall, the smoldering cigarette glowing as he lifted it nervously to his mouth. She couldn't seem to tear her gaze from him as he reached forward to knock his ashes into the ashtray. She slumped against the back of the couch. Her heart beating rapidly, she couldn't stop more sensual thoughts from exploding into the forefront of her consciousness. Tangled limbs, writhing bodies, clinging mouths, and that final, marvelously full sensation . . . Closing her eyes, she remembered the feel of his sleek shoulders under her hands as he lowered himself to her, and she shook with passionate response.

When he stubbed out his cigarette and turned toward her, she was unable to mask the hunger in her eyes. Slowly he approached and reached out to twist one of her tangled curls around his finger. Looking up at him, she felt as though she were drowning in the flashing purity of his blue eyes as she saw a passion to match her own in their depths.

"We just can't fight this, can we, honey?" he murmured.

His finger left the silky softness of her hair to trail a burning path down her cheek to her throat. There he lingered, as her rapidly beating pulse gave him the answer he sought. She didn't know where she found the strength to push his hand aside, when her entire body ached for his touch.

"Touching me isn't going to solve anything," she said, flinching from him.

"It just might save our sanity," he rasped, his eyes flaring into brilliant demand.

He sounded almost as insecure as she felt, and the thought renewed her confidence. Lifting her eyes to his, she shook her head sadly. "I wasn't out to prove anything with that guy. I wouldn't hurt either of us like that, even if it appeared that way. I danced with him, that's all. He simply drew his own conclusions, Brent. I'm sorry about my behavior at the party, but neither of us should try to pretend it didn't happen. I got drunk and I let some stranger think that I . . ." She hesitated and looked away from him.

"I really showed marvelous maturity, didn't I?" she continued bitterly. "I was hurt, so I indulged in stupid behavior to get even!"

She averted her head, conscious only of the sound of her own breathing, the steady dripping of the faucet she'd neglected to close completely, the clenching and unclenching of Brent's hand at his side. But a more tangible reaction grew in her body when his fingers shaped the contour of her head and coaxed her into meeting his eyes.

"But you wouldn't have gone with him, Joy. That's all that matters, all you should remember," he insisted, his low voice convincingly stern. "We both made accusations in anger. I behaved like an arrogant bastard this afternoon. You were right to be hurt and angry. Like a self-opinionated idiot I took away your freedom of choice and treated you like a child instead of a woman. If it makes you feel any better, I paid for my mistake tonight. God! The mere thought of some guy mauling you is enough to drive me right around the bend.

"You're mine," he whispered, bending down and drawing her to her feet. "You're my woman . . . and only mine."

She reacted to the sensual purr of his voice like a leafy branch swaying in the wind. Her arms wrapped around his neck to steady herself, while her body strained to find the support she needed in his arms. His hands pressed her closer, although he seemed to be holding himself in check. Irritated by the withdrawal she sensed in him, she pushed aside the collar of his shirt and pressed a hot, demanding kiss against his throat.

He jerked as though jolted by an electrical current, and the fingers splayed against her hips dug almost painfully into the twin cushions of flesh. She felt his chest expand with the breath he drew into his lungs; then, with a muffled cry, he lifted her and carried her into the bedroom. It didn't take him long to divest her of her robe, and his eyes drank in the sight of her nakedness as he quickly removed his own clothing.

When his gaze returned to her face, Joy could see the battle that raged behind his half-closed lids. With an entreaty in her own eyes that she made no attempt to mask, she lifted her arms to him. A choked cry erupted from his tightly compressed lips, and then his weight was pressing her into the mattress. She stretched in a movement of both hunger and satisfaction, and the sleek lines of his body merged with hers in elemental fervor.

His mouth became an instrument of torture and the source of unimaginable delight. It slowly and thoroughly sought the most sensitive areas of her flesh with starved insistence. The hard, rosy tips of her breasts, the soft roundness of her quivering stomach, the inside of her thighs. When he parted her legs still wider and his tongue began to taste the essence of her femininity, she gasped and arched her hips to meet his foraging mouth. Sensation built inside of her, until she felt almost maddened with the burning heat of her desire for him. Unable to stand the pleasure-pain of her reaction, she twisted his hair between her fingers and tried to lift his head.

"Let me pleasure you," he whispered, his mouth trailing biting little kisses over the softness of her undulating belly.

"Please," she moaned, her head writhing against the pillow.

"Isn't this what you want?" His teeth gently scoured the inside of her thigh.

Her fingers tightened in his hair with a grip she knew caused him pain. "I want you inside me," she cried.

His head lifted, and her eyes beseeched him to fill the void created by his lovemaking. The lids of his eyes were heavy with passion, his mouth gentle as he refused to respond to her demand. "First let me taste your desire for me."

She closed her eyes, her chest heaving with emotion. "I want to give you pleasure too."

"This does give me pleasure," he said huskily, a smile in his voice. "And I'll make this good for you, babe. I promise I'll make this good for you."

His thumbs parted the moistened curls hiding the treasures he sought, and again his head lowered. Carefully, in slow, sweeping strokes, his tongue laved the tiny bud that had risen at his command. Joy tensed and then shuddered as the liquid heat of her passion spilled over in a convulsive, shattering release. But even as she cried out in an intensity of feeling, she knew it wasn't enough. To satisfy her craving at his expense did nothing to subdue her need to merge herself completely with the man she loved.

She wanted to give as well as receive, and when he lifted himself over her to place a lingering kiss against her parted mouth, her arms and legs trapped him against her arching form. The unconsciously sensual movement snapped the last of his restraint. A primeval cry broke from his throat as he levered her hips into position to receive him, and with a single powerful lunge he buried himself in her welcoming depths.

His hands clenched against the curve of her buttocks as he encouraged her to meet the pounding rhythm of his body, but Joy needed no encouragement. With youthful resilience she was already building toward a greater peak of sensation, her legs tightening around his back to keep him locked in the seat of their passion. Breaking free from all restraint she guided his head to her breast, and felt her mind spinning on a wave of pure ecstasy when his mouth favored first one entreating nipple, then the other.

The gentle suckling motions combined with the smooth stroking of his body between her thighs proved to be the stimulus she needed to seek her completion. Sensing the moment, Brent swallowed with his mouth the sweet cry that erupted from her throat. At the fervent thrust of her tongue against his own, his body went rigid and then demanded its own pleasure, in a moment so poignantly beautiful it brought tears to her eyes.

"Oh, Joy," he whispered, shaking in the arms that held him so tightly. "I love you so much, babe. So much."

"That's all I need," she said, her hands possessively roaming over the dampened flesh of his back and shoulders, "for you to love me."

Brent settled himself beside her and drew her into his arms. "But it's not all I need, Joy."

Snuggling tiredly against his side, she tilted her head back to look at him. Behind the tenderness in his eyes, the masculine satisfaction that still reflected the glory of their lovemaking, was another expression Joy was afraid to leave open to conjecture. "Tell me," she whispered gently.

He traced the quivering lines of her mouth with his forefinger. "I've played the white knight long enough, my lady. I've tried to hold myself back from my own desires where you're concerned, but tonight shot all my resolutions to hell."

"You weren't the only one to learn a lesson," she said softly, placing a kiss on his chest. "Now I realize that I can face anything but losing you. I was willing to fit you into my life, but I was too much of a coward to contemplate fitting myself into yours. But no longer, Brent. I'll give you any kind of commitment you wish, as long as we can be together."

"Despite my career?"

"Despite your career."

"Then, will you marry me, Joy?"

With a muffled cry she threw her arms around his neck. Her words were a soft enticement against his mouth as she sighed, "You just try to stop me, Brent Tyler. You just try!"

The next morning they found Bessie and John in the garden, enjoying the warmth of the golden summer weather. The two of them were seated on the bench of the old wooden picnic table, which had resided beneath the shady branches of the willow tree for as long as Joy could remember.

Bessie spotted them first, and her face creased in a smile of welcome. "Why, hello, you two," she called gaily. "It's about time you paid us another visit, Joy. I was going to ask Brent to bring you to lunch today, but he was so late getting home I finally went to bed."

John Barton carefully extricated his legs from

beneath the table and stood to envelop Joy in a bear hug. He then turned to Brent, his eyes twinkling in his lined face. "What blarney have you been pouring into our girl's ear to make her look so happy, boy?"

Hearing the tall, ruggedly virile man at her side referred to as a boy caused Joy's lips to twitch with suppressed humor. Her effort at self-control was met with a warning glance from Brent, which she blithely ignored. "That's why we're here," she said with a laugh, then planted a smacking kiss on her father's cheek. "He's been promising me all kinds of things, and I wanted you two to stand witness. I'm don't want him to try to back out of this later!"

Brent stepped forward, clearing his throat. He looked so ridiculously uncomfortable, Joy took pity on him, and left the shelter of her father's arms to return to his side. Without saying a word, she smiled up at him.

His features miraculously softened before he straightened his back and returned his gaze to her father. "I've asked Joy to marry me, Dad."

To Joy's dismay John frowned and crossed his arms over his chest. His eyes went from one to the other of them consideringly, until his lips finally twitched into a wide smile. "Well, don't leave Mother and me in suspense," he bellowed, motioning for his wife to join them. "What did she answer?"

" 'Yes,' " Brent muttered, a flush rising in his cheeks.

With a choked cry Bessie hurtled herself into Brent's arms, her eyes filling with tears as she hugged him. "Oh, my darlings." She sniffled, and turned to pull her daughter close. "We're so happy for you both. Dad and I were beginning to think you two would never come to your senses."

Joy gave Brent a smug look before grinning impishly at her mother. "I came to my senses long ago. Brent was a little harder to convince."

Bessie eyed her foster son contemplatively. "I know how stubborn he can be," she teased, her plump cheeks pinkening prettily. "However did you manage, dear?"

Joy pursed her lips, her eyes twinkling roguishly. "I wore tight pants and low-cut blouses."

"Joy!"

Brent's hissing reprimand was accompanied by the sound of John choking in the background, but Bessie never turned a hair. Her understanding smile held only admiration as she linked her arm through her daughter's. "That's just the way I convinced your father, dear!"

From then on bedlam reigned, as congratulations and questions were thrown at Joy and Brent with a rapidity that left them looking at each other in bewilderment. John disappeared into the house for a moment, and returned with a bottle of chilled champagne and four glasses.

"Dad, you old fraud." Joy laughed, pointing to the wine. "How long have you been saving that?"

He chuckled and handed the glasses to Bessie.

"About a month," he admitted. "I may be getting old, but I'm far from senile. Brent's been like a cat on hot bricks every day while you were at work. If there's one thing I'm qualified to judge, it's a man in love."

He sent a speaking glance toward Bessie, who smiled in return while automatically shushing him. "Get that look off your face, you old reprobate, and pour the wine. I want to toast the future happiness of our son and daughter."

This task accomplished, they soon settled down for a practical discussion of the wedding. Although Bessie was disappointed, Joy was firm in her decision to have a small, intimate ceremony in the corner church she had attended as a child. "After all, Mother," she said, sending Brent a teasing glance from beneath her lashes, "it took all Brent's courage to propose. I think he'd rather face a group of armed terrorists than a church filled with people."

"That just goes to prove his sanity," her father retorted, winking at Brent. "You women, with your pomp and circumstance, have driven many a groom to bolster his courage with a little liquid refreshment. You want Brent to be able to remember his wedding day, don't you?"

"Speaking of wedding days," Bessie said, "exactly what date have you decided on?"

Joy went still at her mother's words and slowly turned her head to study Brent's expression. His face didn't give away a single thought. Their eyes met and held, and Joy felt herself suddenly shivering with repressed tension. There was an air of decision in the hard angle of his jaw, in the way he held his head, and yet she was conscious of a flicker of regret in his eyes as he answered Bessie's question.

"I'd like the wedding to take place as soon as possible, but I'm afraid I've committed myself to another overseas assignment."

Joy clenched her hands in her lap and forced a smile. She was going to begin as she meant to go on, she decided determinedly. She was going to show Brent that she wouldn't allow his career to come between them. "You didn't tell me where you'll be going, Brent."

His eyes narrowed as he told her, and she saw him flinch as the color washed from her face. "But even the United States diplomats and their families have been flown out of there, Brent," she said without thinking. "When the war escalated, the government decided the situation was too explosive for Americans to remain in the area."

"I'm a correspondent, not a diplomat, Joy."

"I know, but—" She stopped abruptly, remembering what she had promised herself, what she had promised Brent.

"But it's so dangerous, Brent," she whispered as fear began to twist her insides.

"I've faced danger before," Brent said, dropping a reassuring arm around her shoulders. "I'll come back to you."

She grasped his words as though they were a lifeline. Both her parents were looking at her with concern, and Brent's hold on her tightened. She would not fail him, she would not. Somehow, somewhere, she would find the strength.

Brent shifted and faced Bess. "We can get married as soon as I get back, Mother," he said. "This will be my last assignment as a correspondent. I've already turned in my resignation."

Joy stiffened with a gasp. She had finally gotten what she'd always wanted, she thought bitterly. Brent loved her, they were going to be married, and he was going to end the career he loved, to provide her with a home and security. He had been strong enough to deny his own feelings when he had tried to tell her he was the wrong man for her. When he had failed in that he had decided to change himself for her. She wouldn't need to find that strength. Brent wasn't giving her the chance to prove herself. They would marry, and she would forever carry the guilt of knowing she was responsible for destroying the career he had so carefully built.

Ten

When Brent unlocked the door to her apartment, Joy brushed past him hurriedly. The tension had grown between them during the ride home, until her attempts to lighten the atmosphere with nonsensical chatter had faded into a silence fraught with all the words that should have been spoken. She knew the path she had chosen to follow, yet she wanted to delay the inevitable confrontation as long as possible.

The controlled slam of the door behind her caused her to jump and glance nervously over her shoulder at Brent. "Would—would you like a cup of coffee?"

"I would like to know what the hell's the matter with you!"

Taking a deep breath, she steeled herself to

respond. Slowly she expelled the breath on a sigh, praying for the proper words she needed to convey her true feelings. "When did you decide to end your career as a foreign correspondent, Brent?"

His mouth twisted wryly. "Don't make it sound like I'm selling my soul to the devil, honey."

"No! But it is the price you're demanding of yourself, isn't it?"

"The price for what?" he asked, the quietness of his voice betraying his frustration.

"For marrying me," she cried, biting down on her lip when she saw the anger leap into his eyes.

"Don't talk like an idiot!"

"I'm not," she nearly screamed, lifting her hand to cover her trembling lips. "You knew I could never be at peace, let alone happy, with you as a foreign correspondent, didn't you? You knew by the way I reacted when you told us about your assignment. Was that when you made your choice, or was it when you made love to me? Now I know you love me more than your work, but you'll never be able to be as sure of me. You took away my own power of choice by your protective attitude, and by doing so, belittled the extent of my love for you."

"All right." He sighed, rubbing the back of his neck. "Maybe all this time I've subconsciously been testing your love, but if I have it's been because of my own feelings of inadequacy, not yours. When I was growing up I went without love for so long I never learned to believe in it. By the time I came to your family and saw loving firsthand, I was too old to feel I was anything but an unnecessary appendage to an already happy home."

He began prowling restlessly around the room, his gaze distracted. "Even though Mother and Dad tried to prevent it, after I left for college I had again reverted to being an outsider looking in. When I came home for visits, you were the only one with the ability to make me feel I still belonged. You seemed to need me, and I never wanted it to change. But you grew up on me, Joy, and you've proved you can make it without me. Because you no longer need me, I had to know you loved me enough to stand by me if the going got rough. I'm not the prince in the fairy tale and I'm not the hero figure from your childhood. I can be hard, and ruthless, and my temper often makes me far from agreeable. But I'll do anything to make you happy, because it would break me if someday you realized you'd made a mistake and turned from me."

He saw the anguish his words caused and in three strides was across the room. His palms were warm and strong against her cold face, but she drew no comfort from his touch. "My shining knight," she murmured, her eyes filling with tears she wouldn't allow to fall.

His hands tightened against her face before he released her. "Joy, I . . ."

With a stifled moan she placed the tips of her fingers against his lips. He searched out and found the sadness in her eyes. His jaw clenched, and he turned away.

"I can't marry you, Brent!" The words tumbled

from her mouth before she could stop them, and her heart closed around the pain caused by her admission.

"I love you, babe."

"I know you do," she whispered. "A long time ago, all I wanted from life was to hear you say those words to me, and to know you really meant them for the woman you loved. But you were right when you told me that what we think we want isn't always good for us. I once accused you of playing games, while all along I was the one playing hide-and-seek with the truth."

The harsh intake of his breath convinced her she had said enough, and her voice filtered into silence. Slowly she moved toward the couch, and sat down on its edge. She wanted to cling to him, to show her grief at the hopelessness of their situation. She wanted to beg him to stay with her, but she knew to do so would be a desecration of the love she felt for him. She had to cut the ties that bound them together, and give Brent his freedom.

He knelt in front of her and stroked the side of her cheek. "I don't believe you," he muttered, his face reflecting shock and bewilderment. "We can work it out if we both try."

His palm felt the shake of her head, and with a groan he leaned forward and pressed his mouth against the soft hair at the side of her neck. She grasped the front of his shirt. Although muffled against her hair, his voice held desperation as he drew her more closely to his body.

"Since I received the Pulitzer nomination for

my work in Ireland last year, I've gotten a lot of job offers, Joy. Until recently, none of them appealed to me. But now I—"

What she had feared most was happening, and with a quiver of rejection she withdrew from his arms. "Don't make any sacrifices for me," she whispered hollowly.

"Damn it," he muttered, rising to his feet to tower over her. "There wouldn't be any sacrifice involved. I want to—"

"But I can't, Brent," she cried, her eyes filling with pain. "I really can't!"

She was losing him, but she had little choice. They couldn't enter into a marriage with each of them expecting the other to change. She had foolishly thought their love enough to magically settle their disparate dreams for the future, when in actuality the ties that bound them would spell destruction for all they valued in each other.

Brent reached down and gently ran his hand over her hair. "There's nothing left for us?"

He didn't wait for an answer. His hands shook as he groped beside her for his jacket. Then he turned, and she saw his broad back flex from the deep breath he drew into his lungs. He walked away, slowly, and she felt sick with the finality of his actions as the door opened.

Her lips were tightly compressed as she forced herself to cross the distance separating them. She didn't know the answer to his question, so she said the only thing she knew was true. "I'm so sorry, Brent."

Her strained whisper reached him. He hesitated, his own eyes clouding with pain as he watched tears slowly trickle from her eyes. The look on his face told her all she needed to know. The chasm had split fully apart, and now they each stood alone on opposite sides.

"Don't cry," he murmured, brushing at her tears with the tips of his fingers. "It wasn't your fault we couldn't make it together, babe."

"Oh, Brent, I . . ."

He shook his head, his smile filled with grief for all they had lost. "No regrets," he whispered, a firm finger lifting her face to his gaze. "I think it'll be better for both of us if I stick to my original plans and leave in the morning. But will you promise me something, Joy?"

She nodded.

"You no longer feel you can marry me, and I'll have to accept that. But I'm still a man who loves you. You're very much a part of my life, and I don't want to lose you entirely. Will you write to me, babe?"

"I'll write," she said in a choked voice, and laid her hand against his arm. "But you'll have to promise to come home to visit between assignments. I—I couldn't stand it if you stayed away another four years because of me. This is where you belong."

He shook his head. "I don't belong anywhere, Joy," he said softly. "I never have."

"Please . . . promise me, Brent."

"I'd just have to go away again," he said

harshly, running his hand through his hair. "God, I don't know if I . . ."

She closed her eyes against the pain. Yes, he would always go away, this man she loved to the exclusion of everything else in her life . In her heart she must have known the day would come when he would leave, but she couldn't bear that knowledge. She had to be left with something to cling to. She felt his hands press against her temples, the stillness in his fingers making his tension obvious.

"One more favor from my lady?" he whispered.

She nodded again and wrapped her arms around his waist. His mouth demanded nothing and gave everything. But as she responded to the sweetness of his lips, she was struck by the realization that he hadn't said he would return. Inwardly she winced with anguish at the thought that this might be the last time she saw him. With a sob she tightened her hands.

He wrenched himself out of her arms, and she was left standing alone. "Brent!"

"Don't say good-bye," he muttered, his eyes lingering on her face before he turned away. "There've been too many good-byes in my life, forever girl."

It was barely dawn when Joy slowly paced beside the river, the sound of her footsteps muffled by the damp grass. She had spent what was left of the night huddled on the couch, a fist shoved against her mouth to stifle the grief that erupted from her in spasms of tears. Eventually she had succumbed to fitful dozing, the passing time distorted by an inward misery that seemed to have no beginning and no end.

Behind her, water dripped from branches and leaves, as though even the trees wept for her. The rustling sound they made overhead matched her mood. It had rained during the night, and the scent of dampened earth saturated the cool breeze. Fall would soon be here in earnest, she thought, and then winter. Slate-colored clouds obliterated the rising sun, and the occasional glimpses of blue were too fleeting to hold much hope for better weather.

She knew why she was here, in a place that spoke to her of Brent. A lump of emotion lodged in her throat as she stared at the scene before her. Now she understood why he had always been drawn to the river. How often had he compared its troubled surface to his own life? Fast-paced, the river flowed inevitably forward, always moving, gathering force and strength as it traveled on its long journey.

Tucking her cold hands into the pockets of her jeans, she moved away from the bank. She lowered herself wearily to the ground and drew up her knees to shield herself from the worst of the wind. Dampness filtered through her clothing, but she welcomed the discomfort. It was tangible, something she could understand and absorb into herself. The chilling, moisture-laden breeze was real against her skin, and this morning she desperately needed the reassurance of familiar sensations.

She had come here rather than give in to the cowardly urge to go to Brent. To alter the course he had set for his life would be to destroy an essential part of the man she loved, and she couldn't allow that to happen. To change him would be to lose him eventually anyway. Though she knew he loved her, she couldn't help but wonder how long it would have taken until he came to hate the restrictions marriage would have placed on him.

Brent knew her so well, she thought, and the face she lifted to the bleak sky reflected the pain of self-realization. He had known she wasn't capable of withstanding the uncertainties of his life, the worry for his safety, the long hours waiting for him to come home. She had finally been shocked from her selfish preoccupation, but realizing she had had the emotional strength to salvage what she could of their relationship left her little consolation.

Her eyes misting, she caught sight of a tree across the river, its trunk buried deeply in the earth. It stood proud and tall, its sturdy branches outlined by the troubled sky. She stiffened, a muffled gasp escaping from her lips. She was like that tree, she thought suddenly. Although it was secure in its resting place, she knew its roots reached beneath the soil and sipped from the passing waters. Without the river, the tree would wither and die.

With a cry she jumped to her feet, her heart pounding in her chest. *Dear God, what have I done?* Without Brent's presence flowing through her life, she too would be dead to everything that made life worth living. What good were the roots of a home to her if she would remain alone, thirsting for the man she loved? Brent's words echoed hauntingly in her mind. "I don't belong anywhere, Joy. I never have."

"I never have . . . never have . . ." But he had! Joy whirled and began running through the damp, tangled weeds surrounding her, back to her car. They belonged to each other and always would. From the very beginning he had found his home in her. Home was more than wood or mortar. It was a place of love and warmth, and its real foundation was built on people, not places. Understanding now that elemental truth, she knew she could endure long separations from Brent. He would always leave a part of himself behind to strengthen her. Or she could wander the world with him, secure in the knowledge that the only home she needed was in his heart.

Finally reaching her car, she threw open the door and scrambled inside. Her hand shook as she pushed the key into the ignition and she quickly started the engine. She depressed the accelerator with a surge of impatience and moistened her lips with the tip of her tongue. She turned onto the old Sacramento bridge with a sigh of relief. As she caught a glimpse of the swirling waters below, she felt a lump in her throat. She was going home . . . to Brent!

She screeched to a halt in front of her old home, her pulse rioting out of control. Her father's pickup was parked in the driveway, but there was no sign of Brent's rental car. "Don't be gone," she whispered. "Please still be here."

Her voice sounded overloud as she skirted the lawn, and approached the front door. Her stomach clenched with fear, and she rubbed her perspiring palms against her jeans before she reached for the doorknob. But the cold metal slid against her fingers as she twisted it in her hand. After wasting several moments in useless mutterings, she finally managed to perform the simple task. The faint murmur of voices reached her when she entered the hall, and she hurried toward the sound.

She stopped abruptly at the entrance to her father's den and stared at her parents in disbelief. John Barton was leaning heavily against the bar, his head bowed as he stared down at the drink in his hand. Bessie sat hunched over in her husband's big leather chair, her hands covering her face. It was her mother's presence in the room that broke Joy free of her shocked immobility. That her mother was there, while her father stood drinking in the early morning at the bar that had been a constant source of irritation between them, caused Joy's mouth to dry with apprehension. Her father looked up as she stumbled across the threshold.

"Where's Brent?" she gasped.

John's head moved in an ominously slow negative gesture, his eyes filled with pity when he saw his daughter's ravaged features. "He's gone, honey."

She clenched her fists and walked stiffly over to her mother. Bessie lowered her hands, revealing the tear tracks on her face.

"Mother?" It was a plea for comfort, and Bessie's arms reached out to draw Joy against her breast.

"What went wrong, darling?" Bessie whispered, her voice thick with emotion. "Brent told us the two of you had decided you'd made a mistake. He tried to reassure us, but—" Her breath caught on a sob. "Oh, Joy! I just don't understand what could have happened. You were so happy together."

"I sent him away," Joy cried, pulling herself out of her mother's arms.

"But why?"

"That doesn't matter now," she said harshly. "What matters is letting him know I was wrong."

"Are you certain you *were* wrong to end things, Joy?" John asked.

She turned and crossed the room to him. She nodded as she slipped her arms around his ample waist. "I've got to go to him, Dad. Please help me."

He patted her back, and when she glanced up at him she saw the relieved smile he exchanged with her mother. "We know you do, honey. He needs you, and your mother and I have always known how much you need him."

Bessie joined them, and pressed a crumpled piece of paper into Joy's hand. "This is where he'll be staying until he leaves on his assignment. You both have our blessing, and our love."

John's voice vibrated with its usual resonance as he hugged Joy and walked toward the kitchen. "I'll call and arrange for the earliest flight to Chicago. You go home and pack a bag, and Mother and I'll pick you up and take you to the airport."

The next few hours were filled with activity, and it was only as she said good-bye to her parents in the departure lounge of the Sacramento airport that Joy had time to feel nervous. What if she arrived to find Brent had already left? She hugged her parents and almost ran to the boarding gate before her courage could desert her. Take one thing at a time, she silently admonished herself.

The flight was long, and far from restful. She was unable to swallow much of the meal the airline provided, and by the time the plan landed she was exhausted. The night without sleep, coupled with the tremendous emotional upheaval of the last several hours, had left her with a nagging ache in the back of her head. She saw nothing of the passing city as the taxi took her to her destination, her mind completely preoccupied with thoughts of what awaited her.

When she entered the foyer of the luxurious high-rise hotel, Joy simply smiled at the man behind the registration desk. She already had Brent's room number, and didn't consider stopping to have him called from the desk. She preferred to land on his doorstep like an unexpected package rather than involve a stranger in their reunion.

The heavy elevator doors closed behind her,

and, clenching her teeth, she stared fixedly at the numbered lights overhead that indicated the passing floors. Her stomach lurched at the swiftness of her ascent, and she felt stifled by the enclosed area. As the doors opened to disclose a long, gray-carpeted hallway, she sighed with relief. It didn't take her long to locate Brent's room, but she wasted precious minutes calming herself before knocking on the door.

It opened almost instantly, and Brent stared at her, speechless for a moment. "Joy, what are you doing here?" he asked when he found his voice.

Her thoughts were whirling around in her head, and she couldn't gather them sufficiently to answer him, so she simply brushed past him into the room. The door slammed shut behind her, and, startled, she dropped her suitcase. Turning to face him, she swallowed at the harshness lining his features. His hair, she noted with an ache, was plastered to his head from a recent shower. His white shirt was almost entirely unbuttoned, tucked carelessly into snug-fitting jeans. His potent sensuality blocked any words of greeting she might have uttered.

He ran a hand over the back of his neck, and she smiled at this single, endearing sign of his nervousness. His gaze lingered on the gentle curve of her lips, and his eyes softened as he raised them to hers.

"Why are you here, Joy?" he repeated, his voice husky with appeal this time. The wariness in his expression caught at her heart, since she knew she was the cause of it.

"I'm here because I needed to see you again," she said softly.

He strode swiftly across the room and dropped down on the couch. She sat next to him and glanced around with assumed interest. "This is a beautiful room," she said.

"Dear God, Joy!" he muttered, brushing his hair back with a shaking hand. "Don't draw this out."

She tentatively touched his arm. "I forgot to tell you something before you left, and it needs to be said."

He lowered his head, apparently fascinated by the sight of her slim fingers against his white sleeve. She pressed her advantage and slowly moved her hand in a simple caress. She heard the intake of his breath as her touch lingered.

Trembling, she leaned her head against his shoulder and looked directly into his eyes. "It's just that I can't live without you."

His jaw clenched briefly before he spoke. "Then, why did you make me think you'd changed your mind about the way you felt?"

"For the same reason you were so ready to believe me, Brent. We were both so busy manufacturing potential problems, we forgot to trust in the strength of our love for each other. I was afraid of making that final commitment because I decided you needed your freedom more than you needed me," she whispered. "I was wrong, wasn't I?"

"I could never be free of you," he replied, his eyes revealing all the love she could wish for. "I thought you knew that."

"We've both spent so much time making assumptions, I'm amazed we ever got around to making love," she teased.

"Making love," he mused, pressing her cheek more firmly against his shoulder. "That's such a beautiful phrase."

He took a deep breath. "You're the only joy in my life. Without you, nothing means anything to me. I don't want to wander the world, when I know that everything that's important to me is at home with you."

"You don't have to give up your career to have what you want, my love. I'll go with you when I can, or wait for you to come back to me. Just as long as we have each other, we'll be happy."

His laughter held the echoes of deep emotion. "You might be willing to spend so much time away from me, but I'm certainly not going to let you out of my sight very often. I never told you about that job I've been offered. I've already accepted, so this really will be my last assignment as a journalist. I'm to host a monthly television documentary series on world affairs. I'll still have to travel a bit, but not for any length of time. Will you mind marrying a television personality and moving to Los Angeles?"

She sat up, her mouth opening in surprise and delight. "Los Angeles?" she squeaked. "Oh, Brent!"

He grinned. "I wouldn't want my clever little wife to give up her own career. You'd spend all our married life calling me a chauvinist. This way, you can accept that promotion. We'll both have what we want, babe."

She lowered her lashes to hide a lingering doubt. "Are you certain that is what you want, Brent? Because I—"

A gentle finger stilled her words. She looked up and was struck by the sincerity in his eyes. "I'm tired of having to go it alone, Joy. I would have discussed it with you before, but I wasn't certain the job was mine and I didn't feel it was fair to raise your hopes. A special-delivery letter was waiting for me when I got home last night, and before I left this morning I called the television station to accept the position."

"Then why did you leave without explaining all of this to me?"

"Because I've never taken your love lightly, Joy." He hesitated, as though coming to a decision. "When you made me think you wanted out of our relationship, I thought you were trying to avoid telling me that you—"

"That I'd mistaken my feelings?"

He nodded, his eyes brooding. "I've never had much faith in my ability to hold on to the people who mattered to me," he admitted quietly. "When I was five, my mother placed me in a county home. I never saw her again, and until you came along, the word love had lost all meaning for me."

"And now?"

"By the time I got on that plane, I'd already called myself every kind of a fool. I decided to give you enough time to realize that I hadn't changed the direction of my career as some kind of penance, and then I was going to go home and try again."

She smiled with deliberate provocation. "Just what kind of a battle plan had you thought up, Mr. Tyler?"

He grinned, his body pressing her against the back of the couch. "I was going to seduce you back into my bed and make love to you until you decided you couldn't do without me."

She moistened her lips with the tip of her tongue. "I've already admitted I can't do without you. Does that mean you're not going to entice me into your bed?"

His eyes darkened, and he stood and lifted her into his arms. "What do you think?"

As he carried her into the bedroom, Joy curled against him, seeking all of his warmth and vibrancy. Her hands tightened around his neck, and when he smiled down at her, her eyes glowed with the intensity of her love for him. With a satisfied murmur she pressed a kiss against his throat, and felt his body tremble. They were in each other's arms, where they belonged, she thought euphorically, where they would always belong. They had searched the heart of their love and found trust, understanding, and acceptance of each other's needs. They had come home!

THE EDITOR'S CORNER

Imagine the dark night sky on the Fourth of July with myriad fireworks going off—exciting skyrockets buzzing through the air, and wheels of dazzling colors exploding in the dark heavens. We've tried to give you a LOVESWEPT celebration for Independence Day that matches those fireworks in exciting and beautiful reading entertainment.

To start our July "display" we have another real dazzler from Sandra Brown in LOVESWEPT #51, **SEND NO FLOWERS.** As always, Sandra gives us a wonderfully satisfying love story. Do you remember the dear, clinging Alicia from **BREAKFAST IN BED,** LOVESWEPT #22? She was the lady who inadvertently caused the torment that kept Sloan and Carter apart. Well, now Sandra has had Alicia grow up and become an independent woman and an excellent mother for her two boys. Still, though, love has eluded Alicia. But, in **SEND NO FLOWERS,** Alicia meets the man she's never even dared to dream of finding. Alicia has taken her sons on a camping trip when a violent thunderstorm blows up. Just what a mother alone needs, right? Then the devastatingly attractive and gently caring Pierce Reynolds charges to the rescue. Just what a mother alone needs, for sure! Pierce not only saves the family's camping trip, but brings a completeness to Alicia's life that she has never known before. Pierce has a terrible secret, though, and it threatens his and Alicia's new found love. The conclusion of this shimmeringly sensual love story is so highly dramatic and emotionally touching that I suspect you will long remember **SEND NO FLOWERS.**

(continued)

Isn't it interesting to read a love story that's the product of a collaboration between a happily married husband and wife? Think back to **LIGHTNING THAT LINGERS** by Sharon and Tom Curtis, for example. I trust you'll find a special quality of romance in Liv and Ken Harper's first romance for us, **CASEY'S CAVALIER,** LOVESWEPT #52. In this charming book, heroine Casey O'Neil pulls every trick in the book to evade process server Michael Cooper . . . even to faking a heart attack and donning clever disguises. She'll stop at nothing to keep from appearing in court. But nowhere has there ever been a more determined (or heroic!) pursuer than Michael. (He's quite a determined wooer, too!) Casey's and Michael's zany pursuit toward love is like a string of firecrackers going off in this fast-paced love story. You've read the romances by Liv and Ken under the pseudonyms of Jolene Adams (SECOND CHANCE AT LOVE) and JoAnna Brandon (ECSTASY) and now you can enjoy **CASEY'S CAVALIER** published at last under their real names.

You've heard me say it before, but it bears repeating: it's an enormous pleasure for editors to find a brand-new writing talent and publish an author for the very first time. Making her debut as a published author next month is Barbara Boswell with LOVESWEPT #53, **LITTLE CONSEQUENCES.** In this delectable romance Shay Flynn knows that blueblood lawyer Adam Wickwire would make a perfect father for the baby she longs to have . . . but marriage is out of the question—for poignant reasons. So, she makes up her mind to seduce Adam, then vanish forever from his life. When the weekend they spend together leaves her breathless—and more than a little in love—Shay discovers that her perfect plan has resulted in some very, very interesting **LITTLE CONSEQUENCES!** (#53)

A month with a romance by Joan Domning is a month with an extra ray of sunshine! In LOVESWEPT #54, **THE GYPSY AND THE YACHTSMAN,** Joan has outdone herself once more. When heroine Tanya Stanchek's horoscope predicts that "romance will crash into you," she hasn't a clue it's going to happen . . . literally! Then a speeding car smacks into hers and tosses the ruggedly handsome Gene Crandall into her path. But a charmingly offbeat fortuneteller, Madame Delores, a mysterious yachtsman whom Tanya has only glimpsed from afar, Gene's biases, and her own anxieties jeopardize the "destined" romance of these two wonderful people. Joan has brewed a delicious stew, seasoned with just the right spices and lots of touching emotion, and I'll bet you agree with me that this is one of her most creative "recipes" for love!

Have a wonderful month of lazy, happy July days brightened up even more by our LOVESWEPT "fireworks."

Warm regards,

Carolyn Nichols

Carolyn Nichols
Editor
LOVESWEPT
Bantam Books, Inc.
666 Fifth Avenue
New York, NY 10103